THE PROMISED YEAR

by the same author

THE DANCING KETTLE
and Other Japanese Folk Tales

THE MAGIC LISTENING CAP
More Folk Tales from Japan

TAKAO AND GRANDFATHER'S SWORD

The Promised Year

YOSHIKO UCHIDA

Illustrated by William M. Hutchinson

HARCOURT, BRACE & WORLD, INC., NEW YORK

My thanks to Mr. Joe Oishi who taught me many things about carnation growing at his nursery in Richmond, California.

Y.U.

E.11.66

Library of Congress Catalog Card Number: 59-9270
Printed in the United States of America

For Michiko

Contents

Contents

THE PROMISED YEAR

1

Something to Be Curious About

Keiko stood at the railing of the freighter and pulled the collar of her new red wool coat up around her ears. She flopped her braids back out of the way and squinted hard at the land that slipped away into the cold gray mist. She rubbed her eyes, but it was no use; the slate roof tops of Yokohama were fading into the mountains and the mountains themselves were melting into the murky November sky. No matter how hard she looked, Japan grew smaller and smaller as the *Nikko Maru* pushed out toward the Pacific. Keiko sniffed, and then, because she knew no one was watching, she wiped her nose with the back of her hand.

Maybe she had made a horrible mistake to say she would go to America. Maybe Aunt Emi and Uncle Henry would be terrible to live with. Maybe she would be sorry she ever left home. It had seemed such a wonderful idea six months ago when the letter had come. Mother had unfolded the thin blue air letter with Aunt

Emi's spidery handwriting dancing down the page.

"Your family is now without a father and you have many mouths to feed," she read. "We have no children, and milk and butter are plentiful in California. Why don't you send one of your children to live with us for at least a year —perhaps longer?"

Her big brother, Hiro, had been the first to speak. "I'll go," he said in a loud voice. "Let me go."

But Grandmother had been firm. "What are you thinking about, Hiro?" she had asked almost crossly. "You are the eldest son. You must stay and carry on your father's name. Who will help your mother deliver flowers from the shop if you go?"

That was when Keiko had spoken. "I'm ten," she had said. "I'm next oldest. Let me go." Besides, she was best in English of anyone at home or even at school.

Hana, although she was only five, felt obliged to say something too. "Shall I go?" she had asked in a voice so small they could scarcely hear. Only Kenbo had been silent because he was just three and he didn't understand.

Keiko could understand well enough. If she

went to America to eat butter and eggs at Aunt Emi's house, there would be that much less for Mother to buy in Tokyo.

"I'll go," she said again. Then the idea of sailing on a ship and living in America began to seem like an exciting thing. "Let me go," she urged.

"Only if you truly want to," Mother said gently. "I want you to be sure."

Keiko nodded. "I'm sure," she said brightly, and she had begun to have a tiny thread of doubt only when Mother added, "Well, I suppose living away from home will be a good test of your character. Perhaps, if you are a very good daughter to them, Uncle Henry will ask you to stay and send you through school."

"But won't I ever come home?" Keiko had asked, alarmed. She hadn't planned on that.

Mother put an arm around her shoulder. "Of course you will, Kei-chan," she had said, "whenever you want to. But I want you to be the one to decide. I don't want Aunt Emi to send you home because you failed to be a good daughter. I want them to be proud of you, even if you stay only a year."

Of course she would stay only a year. Keiko promised herself deep in her heart that she would stay no longer than that. By the time the rice fields turned gold and the threshers began to hum, she would be back in Tokyo again. It made her feel almost lightheaded to think of the fun she would have bringing home presents for everyone and telling her class about America. It wouldn't be any trouble at all to write an interesting composition for class then, and she would not have to write of such things as visiting Father at the sanitarium or Hana's having fallen into the lake at Ueno Park.

Once it was settled that she should go, Keiko could scarcely wait for all her papers to come. Mother and Grandmother bought her a new suitcase and made her three new dresses. Then she had gone to say good-by to her aunt and uncle in Shibuya, and on the day before she sailed, she had gone for a last visit to Father's grave to tell him she would be gone. "Only for a year," she said firmly.

Now, here she was on the great pale green ship, sailing away from Japan all alone. The world around her suddenly seemed so vast and enormous that Keiko felt about as big as the one-inch boy who, in the old story, sailed the river in a soup bowl.

Keiko looked up at the sky full of the threat of rain and thought of the laundry hanging on the bamboo poles in their yard. If only she were home right now, she thought, she would have run out to gather it in, even before Mother had to ask her.

She watched as the purser unwound the colored paper streamers the wind had tangled around the railing. They had fluttered so gaily for a while, linking Keiko to each hand that waved from the pier. But now, they were only bleak, straggling scraps of paper, as limp as her own brave hopes. She sighed and felt a great sadness creeping over her.

The purser glanced at her with a worried frown. "Look at the gulls, Kei-chan," he said, pointing to the sky. "They'll be dropping behind soon, and we'll have albatross following us once we're out at sea."

Keiko nodded, but she didn't really care. She looked back once more toward Japan, but it was dwindling into a black hump at the rim of the sea. Keiko almost wished her year in America were over and that she was sailing back to Yokohama, her suitcases bulging with presents.

And then she heard a voice behind her.

"*Mah,* why do you stay out in the cold so long? You mustn't stand there looking back at Japan. Look ahead! Look toward America!"

Keiko turned and saw Mrs. Miyagawa who had the cabin opposite hers. She was the only other passenger on the freighter, for not many people liked to travel in November. The first thing she had told Keiko when they met was that she must call her Auntie Kobe just as her nieces did. "You see, they have so many aunts," she explained. "One in Osaka, one in Tokyo, and one in Kyoto. I am the one from Kobe." Keiko knew right away she would like her.

Auntie Kobe peered over her glasses at her now, just as Grandma often did. She had the same round, plump face and the graying hair pulled into a tight bun in back.

"But I *was* thinking about America, Auntie Kobe," Keiko answered. "Really I was."

Auntie Kobe tipped her head to one side. "Ah so?" she asked. "And what was it you were thinking?"

Keiko paused. "I was thinking how nice it will be to come home from America. I . . ."

"There, you see!" Auntie Kobe interrupted, wagging a finger under her nose. "That is not a constructive thought at all. You haven't even gone and already you are thinking of returning.

"That isn't right at all, is it?" she asked the purser, and she went right on without giving him a chance to answer. "From now on, you and I must think about becoming Americans," she said.

Keiko looked at Auntie Kobe in her purple silk *kimono* with a gray knitted shawl pulled tight around her shoulders. She looked down at the white *tabi* and *zori* she wore on her feet. "You don't look American, Auntie Kobe," she said.

Auntie Kobe clapped her hands together as though she had just had a marvelous idea. "Come with me to my cabin," she said eagerly. "I will show you a real American dress I have. *Sah,* come along."

The purser hurried ahead to open the heavy door for them. "Luncheon will be served in an hour," he said, as though to caution Auntie Kobe against opening too many suitcases. But Auntie Kobe scarcely paid any attention to him.

"Yes, yes . . . all right," she murmured, and taking Keiko by the hand, she hurried down the narrow corridor that led to her cabin. She took the key from her sleeve and unlocked the door.

"Now, wait outside," she said to Keiko. "I'll only be a minute."

Keiko leaned against the closed door and wondered why Auntie Kobe had done that. Perhaps she was going to surprise her by putting on a western dress before she let her in. Keiko stood stiff and straight against the door, practicing the posture exercise she'd learned at school. Stomach in . . . chest out . . . shoulders straight.

She nearly fell in backwards when Auntie Kobe opened the door. "Now," she said, "come in."

Keiko turned to look at Auntie Kobe, but she was still dressed exactly as she had been before. She breathed heavily and murmured, "*Mah,* such a struggle." But when Keiko asked her what she was talking about, she simply spoke of something else.

"Now, I shall show you my American dress and shoes," she said proudly, and kneeling to the floor, she pulled two bulging brown leather suitcases from beneath her bunk. Then she sat beside them, just as though she were sitting on the floor matting at home.

"Come," she said, pointing to the floor where she wanted Keiko to sit. Taking a tiny key from her pocketbook, Auntie Kobe unlocked both suitcases and spilled their contents out on the floor. Keiko felt as though she'd suddenly been thrown into a sea of *kimonos,* brocade sashes, and sandals, and the smell of moth balls tickled her nose and made her sneeze.

"My goodness!" she said. She had never seen so much come out of two small suitcases.

Now Auntie Kobe's hands fluttered over everything like a pair of butterfly wings, sorting and choosing, making little piles of things that had filled her bags. Keiko watched, fascinated. It was like watching a vendor setting up shop at a temple stall for a festival night. Besides all her clothing, there were silk scarfs and wool shawls and embroidered handkerchiefs trimmed with crocheted edges. There were wooden clogs and straw sandals, and from inside a pair of black shoes tumbled a string of prayer beads wrapped in red silk. There were small white candles, boxes of incense, an incense burner made of brass, three books, a Japanese-English dictionary, and a half-dozen tins of green tea, dried seaweed, salt rice crackers, and sugared beans. "For presents," Auntie Kobe explained, pointing to the tins.

From the pockets of the suitcases came more

things. There were a string of pearls in a box of purple velour, a dozen packages of plasters for backaches, a package of hairpins, two hair nets, a bottle of camellia hair oil wrapped in a piece of plastic, an old rice-cracker tin filled with medicine, white *tabi,* and three pairs of nylon stockings. At the very bottom of one of the suit-cases, there were two sweaters that Auntie Kobe had knit herself, a navy-blue wool skirt, and at last, a dress of gray wool with a row of but-tons running down the front.

"Did you bring everything in your house?" Keiko asked.

Auntie Kobe chuckled and her round shoul-ders shook. "Ah, if you only knew what I brought," she began.

"What?" Keiko asked quickly. "What did you bring?"

But Auntie Kobe wasn't telling. She kept her half-finished sentence to herself and drew out the gray dress to show Keiko. When she shook it out, a white envelope fell from its folds.

"Ah, here is Jiro," she said, and taking out a photograph, she held it up for Keiko to see. "This is my son," she said gently. "He is the rea-son I am going to America."

Keiko looked at the picture and saw a solemn-faced boy in a black high-school uniform. A long scar crossed his right cheek, and he looked as lonely as a starless winter night.

"He won't be lonely any more when you come, will he?" she asked.

But Auntie Kobe simply shook her head. "I must find him first," she said dismally. And then she told Keiko her long sad story, the words tumbling from her lips like rice boiling over from a pot. She told how there had been too many boys who wanted to enter the university and how Jiro could not get in. She told how sad he had been and how, one day, he had simply sailed away on a freighter.

"He said he'd be back in a year," Auntie Kobe went on, "but the cherries bloomed and the rainy season came and still he didn't come back. At last, he wrote to me from California and said he would send for me when he was ready. And that was all. He never wrote again."

"He doesn't sound very nice," Keiko said, "but I'll help you look for him if you want me to." She studied the photograph carefully so she would know him if she ever saw him on the street. Perhaps one day she would bump smack

into him, and she would go up and tap him on the arm and say, "I know you. You are Jiro Miyagawa!"

"Of course he is older now," Auntie Kobe went on. "It has been twenty years since that picture was taken."

Twenty years! Keiko squinted at the photograph and tried to imagine how Jiro looked now. "Maybe he is fat and bald," she said. "Or maybe he has a big mustache and his hair is gray."

Auntie Kobe laughed. "Does forty seem so very old to you?" she asked. "How old did you say you were?"

"I'll be eleven next June," Keiko said, trying to sound like eleven already.

Auntie Kobe looked thoughtful. "Hmmmm," she murmured. "Maybe you are old enough to be trusted with a secret . . ." she began. But at that very moment there was a knock on the door. It was the cabin boy to tell them that lunch was served.

"What secret?" Keiko asked now, for Keiko liked secrets and secret societies better than anything—except maybe chocolate ice cream. In fact, she and her best friend at school were the only members of a secret society that, unfortunately, had to be disbanded because Keiko left. Now maybe she and Auntie Kobe could form a new one of their own. "Tell me, Auntie Kobe," Keiko begged. "Please tell me before lunch."

Auntie Kobe simply got to her feet, however, and answered the boy. "Thank you," she called. "We shall be there presently." Then, quickly gathering her belongings and piling them in a huge heap on her bunk, she hurried Keiko toward the dining salon. Keiko noticed that she locked the door to her cabin before they left and wondered if there were thieves on the ship too. Mother was always careful about keeping their house locked. But when she asked Auntie Kobe, she just laughed and said, "*Mah,* I hope there are no thieves. It's prying people I'm worried about."

Keiko had a feeling that all of this had something to do with her secret. "What about the secret?" she asked in a hoarse whisper. "Can you tell me now?"

Auntie Kobe simply put a finger to her lips. "Shhhh," she said, and she pattered down the corridor as though she were rushing to a year-end sale. "I could eat three bowls of rice. I am so hungry!" she murmured.

When they got to the dining salon, the purser was waiting for them. He helped them to their places and then sat stiff and straight in his black uniform with the gold buttons and braid. Soon he and Auntie Kobe were busy talking about the ship and about the frozen tuna and the porcelains and the toys and the plywood in the hold, and Keiko didn't have a chance to say another word about the secret. Besides, she knew better than to ask in front of the purser. After all, it wouldn't be a secret if everyone knew.

It was only when Keiko was eating the pink wafers thrust into the top of the raspberry sherbet that she noticed Auntie Kobe's lap. There she was, sitting just as calm as you please, talking about Japan's tuna and fishing industry, when all the while she had half of her salmon steak sitting in the napkin on her lap. Keiko leaned over for a better look.

"Auntie Kobe!" she said. "What are you doing with that sa . . ."

But she got no further. Auntie Kobe suddenly bundled everything up in her napkin, tucked it neatly into her *kimono* sleeve before the purser noticed, and quickly excused herself from the table.

"I do believe I am about to have a terrible headache," she said, rubbing her forehead. "Do excuse me, please," and moving quickly across the room, she disappeared down the corridor.

Keiko wanted to leap out of her chair and run after her, but she wanted to eat her sherbet too. After all, the sherbet wouldn't keep and Auntie Kobe would. She ate the rest of it in big icy spoonfuls and then told the purser she thought she was about to have a headache too.

The purser nodded. "Perhaps you are beginning to feel the motion of the ship," he said politely, and he bowed as she left the table and hurried after Auntie Kobe.

The ship was making creaking noises now as it bucked the winds of the Pacific, and Keiko could feel the swell of the waves beneath. It was almost like climbing slippery hills of sand to run down the corridor to Auntie Kobe's cabin.

Keiko knocked on the door and waited. "Auntie Kobe?" she called softly.

There was no sound, but as Keiko put her ear to the door, she thought she heard Auntie Kobe's voice, gentle and coaxing. This time Keiko knocked harder. "Auntie Kobe!" she called in a loud voice. Still Auntie Kobe didn't come to the door. Instead, she called, "I can't see you for a while, Kei-chan. Come back in a few minutes."

Keiko went back to her own cabin then and sat down on the stiff blue upholstered couch. The world of the ship and the sea and Auntie Kobe and the purser and raspberry sherbet with pink wafers was her world now. Already, Tokyo and her family standing on the windy pier were becoming blurred and dim. There was no more sadness crowding into her heart but only the wonder and excitement of Auntie Kobe and her secret. Keiko swung her legs back and forth impatiently, banging her heels against the couch. How much longer should she wait, she wondered, before going back to find out about Auntie Kobe's secret.

2

Auntie Kobe's Secret

As things turned out, Keiko didn't learn Auntie Kobe's secret, or even see her, for several more days, for the ship began to toss and roll and Auntie Kobe grew seasick almost immediately after she locked herself in her cabin. She didn't so much as poke her nose outside the door. Each morning Keiko stopped to knock on her door and ask how she was, but Auntie Kobe only croaked a feeble, "Not well at all," and she didn't invite Keiko to come in. In fact, she would allow no one at all inside her cabin and tottered to the door only to take a tray of food from the cabin boy three times a day.

Finally, on the day they crossed the international date line and had two Tuesdays in a row, Keiko could stand it no longer. She banged on Auntie Kobe's door with her fist and said, "Auntie Kobe, I'm lonesome. Please come out or let me in." She really didn't expect an answer at all but just thought she'd make a little noise to see what would happen. Then, of all things, Auntie Kobe really did come to the door, and this time she was all dressed and her hair was combed.

"*Mah,*" she murmured, pale and weak. "I hope we don't go through any more storms like that!"

Keiko wanted to take her everywhere. There wasn't a corner of the ship she hadn't explored.

"Shall I take you to the bridge, Auntie Kobe?" she asked. "Or do you want to see the radio room or the engine room? Do you want to see the little shrine in the chartroom to keep us safe on our journey? I know all the officers now." Keiko had so many things stored up to tell Auntie Kobe, she couldn't stop talking.

"Just let me go out on deck and sit on that nice steady bench," Auntie Kobe said wearily, and once she sat down, she refused to move.

Keiko waited and waited for her to say something about her secret. She sat and looked at Auntie Kobe like a dog who knew she had a bone tucked away somewhere in her sleeve. But Auntie Kobe simply sat there inhaling deeply, saying how refreshing the sea breezes were. Keiko couldn't bear it another minute.

"Auntie Kobe, you've got to tell me today," she pleaded. "You said I was old enough to keep a secret. I promise not to tell. Please!"

"Ah, yes," Auntie Kobe said, suddenly re-membering. "I did say I would tell you, didn't I?" She looked at Keiko for a moment and then told her to hold out her hands. "Palms up," she directed, and then she squinted through her gold-rimmed glasses and carefully studied the lines on Keiko's palms.

"Hmmmm," she murmured. "Your character line is good. Strong and dependable."

"Mother says I'm very dependable," Keiko said just to help things along, although in fact Mother had said that only once when Keiko managed to deliver chrysanthemums to a cus-tomer who lived far beyond the end of the elec-tric train line. Keiko remembered how she had found the house on a long, winding street by asking her way at five different shops.

Auntie Kobe thought for a moment, and then she said slowly, "Well, I must confide in you one day before we land. Perhaps today is as good a day as any." Then, rising abruptly, she started for her cabin. "Come along," she said.

Keiko hurried after her and felt the pounding of her heart. What should she say if Auntie Kobe produced a suitcase full of stolen jewels? Maybe she was the leader of a gang of counterfeiters. Maybe she had an accomplice stowed away in the cabin. That would explain the mysterious piece of salmon in her napkin.

They reached the cabin, and Auntie Kobe let Keiko in and then quickly turned the key in the lock. Keiko swallowed hard and felt her face grow hot. She had kept lots of secrets before, but they were only small ones, like Hana's when she had spilled ink on Mother's best crocheted tablecloth, or Hiro's when she had caught him going to a movie on the way home from school. She had never had a grownup confess a secret to her before, and now she felt shivery and almost afraid, even though she could scarcely wait to hear it.

Keiko watched as Auntie Kobe went to the bunk opposite her own and then kneeled down to pull out a cardboard carton from beneath it. So that was where she had hidden her jewels! At least it was not an accomplice who crawled out from beneath the bunk. Keiko saw now that the carton was punched with holes, and as Auntie Kobe lifted up the flaps, she began to murmur gently.

"Now, Tama," she said, "it's time at last to meet Kei-chan."

And she pulled from the carton the most

beautiful black cat Keiko had ever seen. It had yellow-gold eyes, four white paws, a white throat, and the tiniest tip of white at the end of its tail.

"Oh, Auntie Kobe," Keiko cried. So this was why her door was always locked and why she had taken the salmon from the table. "Has she been here all along?" she asked.

Auntie Kobe quickly put a finger to her lips. "Shhhhh," she warned. "Someone will hear you."

"She's so beautiful," Keiko murmured, and taking the cat from Auntie Kobe, she rubbed her cheek against the sleek black fur. Tama was as silky smooth as the satin ribbons Mother used on the special bouquets she made for weddings. She lay quietly in Keiko's arms, purring as though she had known her all her life.

"Look, she likes me," Keiko said happily, and she wanted so much to show everyone on the ship. "Can't we just show her to the purser?" she asked. "He won't tell anyone."

Auntie Kobe threw her hands up in the air. "The purser! *Mah!* Why, if I told him, he'd probably take poor Tama right down into the cold, damp hold and lock her up with all those stiff, frozen tuna. I'm not supposed to have an animal in my cabin at all," she said. "Can I trust you not to tell?"

Keiko thrust out her little finger and locked it with Auntie Kobe's. "I promise," she said. "I'll never, never tell. Shall we prick our fingers and mix the blood?"

Auntie Kobe didn't seem to think all that was necessary. "Never mind," she said. "Just promise. And now that you know about Tama, you may visit me anytime you like. It will be nice to have someone I can discuss my problem with."

Auntie Kobe sat down in a chair, sighed, and reached for her knitting. Keiko sat opposite her with Tama in her lap and stroked her soft, silky back. It was as cozy and peaceful as a winter's night when everyone sat around the *hibachi* and warmed their hands over the coals. Auntie Kobe had just hooked the yarn on her finger and begun to purl a row on her sweater when there was a knock on the door.

"Excuse me . . ." It was the purser. "Is Kei-chan in there with you?"

Keiko jumped to her feet and then became so flustered she shoved Tama right on Auntie Kobe's lap. Of course, Tama landed right in the middle of the yarn and promptly proceeded to get so tangled up in it, it was hard to tell where Tama's tail ended and the yarn began.

"Oh! Oh my!" Auntie Kobe groaned, and then she called, "Just a moment, please. Just a moment."

She looked for one frantic moment at Keiko and then at Tama all tangled up in her yarn, and then she pushed them both toward her bunk. "Get in!" she whispered to Keiko.

"But my shoes," Keiko protested.

"Never mind. Get in!"

And Auntie Kobe thrust Tama, yarn, knitting needles, and Keiko—shoes and all—into the bunk. She flung the quilt over them and whispered, "Close your eyes, and whatever you do, don't let go of Tama. Hold on tight!"

Keiko closed her eyes, hugged Tama for dear life, and held her breath as Auntie Kobe went to the door.

"I'm so sorry to have kept you waiting," Auntie Kobe said calmly, and she opened the door just wide enough to let the purser look in. "Little Kei-chan is not feeling well, and I was just putting her to bed. You see, she doesn't look at all well, does she?"

The purser sounded worried. "Why, she looked fine at lunch," he murmured. "Perhaps she has taken cold. I'll go call the doctor at once."

Doctor! Keiko gasped and squeezed her eyes shut even tighter. What would the doctor say if he came and found that she didn't even have so much as a tiny stomach ache. Keiko clutched Tama closer and wished the purser would go away, for now Tama was beginning to squirm. She wriggled and writhed and scratched and got poked by the knitting needles, and finally she let out a terrible, "Eeeeeooooowwwwrrrr!"

Auntie Kobe tried to close the door. "Poor child," she murmured sympathetically. "She does sound sick, but I do believe it is a stomach ache I can cure with my own medicines. Please don't bother the doctor."

Keiko could hear the purser backing down the hall.

"No, no," he protested. "I'll send the doctor down immediately. The child seems to be in great pain."

Auntie Kobe closed the door just in time, for by now Tama was so annoyed, she scratched and screeched and leaped from the bunk with another terrible yowl.

Auntie Kobe thrust her quickly into her cardboard box and pushed it under the opposite bunk. *"Mah,"* she said with a sigh. "I thought that was the end of our secret for sure." And then she began to laugh. "Did you see the look on his face when he heard Tama? I'm afraid he thinks you are terribly sick!"

Keiko was too worried about the doctor's coming to think it was very funny. "He'll make me take some horrible brown medicine," she said dismally.

It didn't take Auntie Kobe long at all to collect her wits. "Now don't get excited," she consoled. "Leave everything to me."

Then with an air of great efficiency she pulled out her suitcase and rummaged about in its pockets. First she took out a small bottle filled with tiny gold seedlike pills. "Good for all ailments of young children," she announced. Next, she pulled out a tin full of white powders wrapped and folded neatly in squares of thin paper. She pushed up her glasses and read from the tin. "For ailments of the stomach due to overeating and the like." And finally, she produced a bottle of milk of magnesia. She lined the medicine up on the table and even emptied one of the white powders in the washbasin so she would have an empty square of paper.

"There," she said. "I shall tell the doctor you have had all of these, and he won't dare give you another thing."

"Be sure you tell him I had the milk of magnesia," Keiko reminded her.

Auntie Kobe nodded and hurried Keiko toward the bunk once more. "Can't you look a little sick?" she inquired.

Keiko barely had time to take off her shoes and climb into the bunk before the doctor came. She tried rolling her eyes, just as a dying soldier had done in a movie she'd once seen, but it was impossible to do this and watch the doctor too, so she had to stop.

The doctor was just like the one at home. He was cheerful and brisk. He smelled of antiseptic and tobacco, and he did the same horrible things. He took her temperature and felt her pulse. He peered down her throat and poked her stomach and made her giggle. He didn't even wear a uniform, but just came down in a big woolly sweater that smelled faintly of naphthalene. And all the while, Auntie Kobe kept up a steady stream of talk that flowed as smoothly as a pitcher of cream. She told the doctor at least five times that she was sure Keiko would be well in no time at all, and she showed

him over and over again the array of medicine on the table.

The doctor listened quietly and then he sat back, looked Keiko straight in the eye, and said, "Well, if all this medicine hasn't made you sick, I think you'll be able to go to the Captain's *sukiyaki* party tonight."

Keiko stopped trying to look sick. "Party!" she cried. "Tonight?"

"The purser told me he was just coming to tell you about it when he learned you were sick," the doctor explained. "We always celebrate crossing the date line with a *sukiyaki* party."

Keiko remembered now. The purser had told her on the first day out about the *sukiyaki* party when all the officers and even the captain would eat with them. She wouldn't miss that for anything.

"Oh, I'll come," she said brightly. "I'll be there."

Then she saw Auntie Kobe giving her a troubled look, and she leaned back, rubbed her stomach, and added limply, "I mean, I'll try."

Auntie Kobe led the doctor to the door. "I'm sure Kei-chan will be quite well by tonight," she said. "Thank you so much for coming to see her."

The doctor turned to look at Keiko once more. "I think perhaps all she needs is a few quick turns on deck," he said. And then, with a quick bow, he was gone. Keiko wasn't sure if they had fooled him at all.

Auntie Kobe sank into a chair. "Such excitement!" she said with a sigh. "I think I need some rest myself," and popping a half-dozen of the tiny gold pills into her mouth, she climbed into the opposite bunk and closed her eyes.

Keiko climbed out of her own bunk, sat at the table, and watched Auntie Kobe go to sleep. She waited until her breathing was slow and even, and then she tiptoed from the room and hurried outside. How good the salt air smelled! Keiko was so full of Auntie Kobe's big secret, she thought she would burst with the keeping of it. There was beautiful black Tama tucked away in the cardboard carton beneath the bunk, and no one on the whole ship—not the purser or the doctor or even the captain himself—knew about it. Only she and Auntie Kobe! Keiko leaned on the railing and looked up at the sky. It was filled with millions of white humps, as though a thousand sheep were crowding across the gray field of the sky. Keiko felt the fine soft spray of the sea on her face and felt her palms grow moist on the rail.

"I know a secret," she whispered to the wind, and the wind flung her words into the sky, beyond the clouds, and up to the albatross that soared and circled over the stern. "I know a great big enormous secret!" Keiko called down to the white foam that surged and frothed as the ship cut its way through the dark water.

"Is it a good secret?" a voice beside her asked.

Keiko was so surprised that she nearly lost her grip on the railing. She turned, and there, standing beside her, was Captain Sawada himself.

"You scared me!" she blurted out. "I almost fell overboard."

The captain bowed. "Forgive me," he said. "I didn't mean to startle you. I just heard you say something about a secret."

Keiko had to bite her tongue to keep from telling about Tama then and there. Captain Sawada was such a kind, gentle, grandfatherly soul, surely he wouldn't mind if a beautiful black cat slept in a box in Auntie Kobe's cabin. Keiko opened her mouth. "I . . ." she began, and then she shook her head. "I can't tell," she said. "I promised."

The captain looked as though he had something to say. A brief smile flickered at his lips, and then he stopped. He patted her on the head and nodded.

"That's right, Kei-chan," he said. "When someone trusts you with a secret, you must guard it and keep it safe in your heart." He gave her a salute then, as though she were an admiral, and went off toward the engine room, whistling a tune. As Keiko watched him go, she had the very same feeling she'd had when the doctor left the cabin. It was as though the captain wasn't being fooled by anybody either.

3

A Close Call

The night of the *sukiyaki* party turned out to be just about as exciting as the night there had been a fire three houses down and Father had gotten them all up to help throw water on their roof.

The officers had put on their dress uniforms and stood at the long linen-covered table looking like soldiers at attention until Keiko and Auntie Kobe were seated. The smell of scallions and paper-thin slices of beef and bean-curd cakes bubbling in the iron skillet on the table made Keiko think of her birthday and festival day all rolled into one.

On birthdays, Mother let each one choose whatever he wanted most to have for dinner. Hiro usually chose sea bream and red bean rice because he knew that was a manly and festive meal. Hana chose egg custard with chicken, Kenbo chose whatever Hiro chose, and Keiko usually asked for *sukiyaki*. Her birthday came in the midst of the summer rains when the house was damp and dreary, and Keiko liked the feeling of sitting at a table with the *suki-yaki* bubbling and simmering in front of them, even though Mother always said that it was a winter dish. The birthday person always sat in the seat of honor, nearest the alcove, which was where Father used to sit.

And now, tonight, Keiko felt she had the seat of honor in the ship's dining salon, for she was sitting between her two favorite officers—the purser and Captain Sawada. Just the day before, the purser had come running to call Keiko to come quickly. And when she had hurried up the narrow stairs to his quarters, he had pointed to his fish tank, where his guppy was having babies. They had sat and watched for two hours, and then he had shown her his stamp collection and his photograph album and the scrapbook of post cards from every port he'd been to. If only Uncle Henry would turn out to be just like him!

The purser raised his tiny wine cup and said, "Here's to a happy new home in America for Keiko and Miyagawa-san."

"And to finding Jiro-san," the captain added, to which Auntie Kobe, her cheeks pink with excitement, answered, "Ah, you are very kind.

I feel that he is very near." And the way Auntie Kobe talked, Keiko felt as though Jiro-san might be walking down the streets of San Francisco that very minute.

Keiko had just finished the clear broth and put the lid back on the lacquer bowl when the shrill sound of the ship's alarm bell suddenly filled the room. Rice bowls stopped halfway to people's mouths, chopsticks stopped in mid-air, tea was left half-sipped, and before Keiko could ask what was wrong, the officers had all leaped from their chairs. Keiko had never seen people move so fast.

"What's wrong?" she asked.

"What can it be?" Auntie Kobe wondered, still too surprised to move from her seat.

But everyone was too busy rushing for their stations to bother answering either of them. The captain murmured a few serious words to the purser, excused himself, and hurried from the room. Before Keiko knew quite what was happening, the cabin boy hurried to them with their life jackets.

"Better put these on," he urged. "Quickly!"

And that was when Auntie Kobe fainted. She didn't even have time to say she felt faint or that she needed air. She simply slid from her chair like a rag doll and slipped right under the table.

"Auntie Kobe!" Keiko shouted, and she ducked under the table to splash water on her face. The purser quickly got Auntie Kobe and stretched her out on the floor. "Miyagawa-san! Miyagawa-san!" he shouted, trying to rouse her.

All the while, the cabin boy was trying to tie on Keiko's life jacket and was having a terrible time because she wouldn't hold still. "Please," he kept saying, "hold still . . . hold still!"

"I think it might be a fire in the engine

room," the cabin boy said in a low voice to the purser. He hadn't meant for Keiko to hear, but Keiko heard anyway, and the very first thing she thought of was Tama. Suppose the ship was on fire and they had to abandon it? Keiko just couldn't leave poor Tama in that carton under the bunk to sink to the bottom of the sea. And certainly, if Auntie Kobe hadn't fainted, she would have gone right off to get Tama herself.

Keiko felt in Auntie Kobe's sleeve and found the key to her cabin. Then, while the purser

and the cabin boy were busy trying to revive Auntie Kobe, she slipped from the room and ran down the corridor. She sniffed, but there wasn't any smoke yet. All she smelled was the delicious smell of *sukiyaki* that had drifted over the ship. Keiko could hear hurried shouts and the sound of running feet and felt cold shivers race down her back. She wondered if there would be time to get her brand-new suitcase, but of course, Tama came first.

Keiko pushed the key in the lock with trembling hands and had to jiggle it a dozen times before she could unlock the door. If she didn't hurry, perhaps both she and Tama would be left behind.

Keiko rushed into the room calling, "Tama! Tama!" But when she looked under the bunk, the carton wasn't there. She glanced quickly around the room and saw that Auntie Kobe had lifted the carton onto her bunk and let Tama out while they were at dinner.

"Tama!" Keiko shouted. Where in the world could she be? Keiko looked under Auntie Kobe's bunk and even threw back the covers to look inside. She opened the closet door and looked, but all she saw were Auntie Kobe's gray dress and her pair of black shoes. And then, she heard a soft "meowr" over her head. Tama was perched on top of the cabinet above the wash-basin in the corner of the room. Keiko felt panicky. How would she ever get her down?

"Hurry, Tama. It's a fire!" she coaxed, but Tama blinked and twitched her tail as though to say the view was fine and she was perfectly happy right where she was. It was no use. Keiko knew she would have to call the purser, for it was surely better to tell Auntie Kobe's secret than to have poor Tama sink with the ship. Keiko had started back toward the dining salon when she heard the purser himself calling her.

"Here I am," Keiko shouted. "Come help me, please. Hurry!"

The purser came running, but now the worried look was gone, and he smiled as he wiped his face with a handkerchief.

"It was a false alarm," he said, sounding enormously relieved. "A short circuit caused it. Everything is under control now. I've been looking for you."

Keiko stood there pointing up at Tama, ready to shout to the purser to please help get her down. Her mouth was open and the words had almost come tumbling out, when she suddenly realized she didn't have to save Tama at all. Furthermore, she had led the purser right to Tama and had given away Auntie Kobe's precious secret.

"What in the world were you up to?" the purser asked. "You had me worried."

"I was . . . I was trying . . ." Keiko began, and then she saw the purser look up.

"Ah, I see," he said softly.

"It was a secret," Keiko said miserably.

The purser helped Keiko take off her life jacket, but he didn't say anything more about Tama.

"You won't tell the captain?" Keiko asked anxiously.

The purser smiled, but still he didn't say anything. He seemed to be turning the whole thing over in his mind. "Everyone is back at the table now," he said. "Let's hurry and we can have another helping of *sukiyaki*."

But Keiko didn't feel a bit hungry any more. In fact, she would just as soon have stayed away altogether. She didn't want to have to see Auntie Kobe's face when the purser told about the cat in her cabin.

Keiko scarcely dared look at Auntie Kobe when she went back to the dining salon, but Auntie Kobe was cheerfully fanning herself with a big white napkin, murmuring that this was absolutely the very first time in all her life that she had ever done anything so foolish as to faint.

"Imagine! I would have missed all the excitement if there had really been a fire," she said. And then she saw Keiko and wanted to know where she had been and if she was all right.

"Where were you, little one?" the captain asked too. "Is everything all right?"

Keiko nodded, but she knew very well that nothing was all right. Everything was horrible, and it was all her fault.

"Where did you find Keiko?" the captain asked.

Keiko looked down at her lap as the purser answered. "Why, she was back in her cabin, sir," he explained calmly. "She'd just gone back to get her pocketbook."

The captain threw back his head and began to laugh. "Just like a woman!" he said. "Rushing back for her pocketbook when the ship might have been on fire."

Everyone at the table roared with laughter, but Keiko didn't mind at all. She knew Auntie Kobe's secret was safe, and she knew that the purser was a real friend.

4

Landing Day

The night before the ship was to dock, Keiko went to Auntie Kobe's cabin to watch as she stuffed and squeezed her possessions back into her bulging leather suitcases. Then she sat and bounced on them, while Auntie Kobe puffed and shoved and finally got the clasps to lock. When that was done, Auntie Kobe turned to her saying, "Now, what are we going to do about Tama?" It was exactly the way Mother turned to Grandmother to ask what she should do about the carpenter who promised but never came to repair the back door. Keiko felt she should have some comforting and wise answer like Grandmother, but Auntie Kobe made this unnecessary by going right on. "We've got to get her off the ship so she won't be locked up in quarantine," she warned.

Keiko wasn't very sure what quarantine was, but she knew it must be a terrible place, and she agreed that Tama must surely be kept out of it.

"But how will we get her off the ship without anyone's noticing?" Auntie Kobe went on.

Keiko tried hard to think. It wasn't often that anyone asked her for advice. On the contrary, people were always trying to give it to her—like Mother telling her to button up her coat, or Grandmother warning her not to sit in a draft after her bath, or Hiro telling her which move to make when she played checkers with Hana.

"I could hide her under my coat," Keiko suggested.

But Auntie Kobe shook her head. She closed her eyes and rubbed her forehead as though she might somehow squeeze out a bright idea with her plump fingertips. Finally, she shrugged. "Ah, well, never mind," she said. "It's time you got to bed. I shall think of something by morning."

Keiko didn't like at all the going-to-bed part of being on the *Nikko Maru*. At home she had never gone to bed alone. She simply spread her quilt out on the floor matting next to Grandmother and Hana. Grandmother always slept in the middle because she knew Hana and Keiko would poke each other and giggle and whisper for hours if she did not plant herself firmly between them. Keiko had always thought it would be such fun to have her own room, but when, on the first night out, she had gone to bed alone, it hadn't been much fun after all. And tonight, of all nights, she just couldn't bear the thought of going off to bed by herself when there were so many things that were meant to be talked about in the darkness with someone else.

"Auntie Kobe," she said suddenly, "let me sleep in your cabin tonight?"

She half expected Auntie Kobe to say of course not and shoo her off to her own cabin, but Auntie Kobe clasped her hands together and said, "What a marvelous idea! You climb into that bunk over there, and we can talk all night if we please."

That was what made Auntie Kobe so wonderful, Keiko thought as she hurried to her own cabin for her toothbrush and pajamas. She was as old as Grandmother, and yet she could think exactly as Keiko herself did. Soon she was lying in the bunk opposite Auntie Kobe's, and the murmur of their voices drifted back and forth across the darkness of the cabin.

Curled up tight in the warm comfort of her bunk, Keiko thought of Aunt Emi and Uncle

Henry. Tomorrow she would see them at last! She decided she should be very dignified and polite when she first met them. She would bow low and thank them for inviting her to come and live with them. Keiko wondered and wondered what they were truly like. Of course she had seen pictures of them. The one she liked best was the one of their wedding, with Aunt Emi standing stiff and small in her white satin gown, carrying a bouquet of lily-of-the-valley, and Uncle Henry beside her, tall and solemn in a morning coat and striped pants. Keiko knew very well they didn't tend the carnations in their nursery dressed like that, but somehow, whenever she thought of them, that was exactly how she pictured them—beautiful and handsome and rather like strangers in a story book. It seemed odd having an uncle and aunt she had never seen, even though they often sent letters and, at Christmastime, great boxes full of candy and cookies and fruitcake.

"You must think of Aunt Emi just as you do of me," Mother had said before Keiko left. "Remember, she is my older sister and not so very different from me. Be truthful and honest, and, above all, be a good daughter to her."

She hadn't said anything about Uncle Henry

because she had never met him herself. Aunt Emi had just gone off all alone to America to marry him. In those days his name had still been Hisakazu, but somehow, over the years, he had become Henry. "Because his name is so difficult for his American friends to say," Aunt Emi had explained. But this made him seem even more a stranger, and even now, Keiko felt a little afraid of him. Somehow, she had the feeling that he had wanted a son. It was probably Hiro he had really wanted.

"I wonder what he'll be like," Keiko murmured sleepily.

And Auntie Kobe's voice answered back in the darkness, "Don't worry; I shall recognize him no matter where I find him."

Keiko was too sleepy to notice, but Auntie Kobe had not spoken of her Uncle Henry at all. She was dreaming her own dreams, and her thoughts were wrapped carefully around the day when she would find Jiro.

Gracefully the ship rode the swells that rippled out over the ocean from a storm far to the north. It rolled from side to side with slow creaking sounds, and Keiko fell asleep feeling as though she were being rocked in a great wooden cradle by a restless wind.

She woke up in the dim light to find Auntie Kobe peering down in her face. "It's landing day, little one," she whispered. "Today we shall be on American soil. Imagine! And listen, I have thought of a way to get Tama off the ship."

Keiko tried to rub the sleep from her eyes. It was bewildering to be told so many important things all at once when she was only half awake. She yawned, stretched down to see how far her toes would reach, and asked sleepily, "Is it morning already?"

"Of course it's morning," Auntie Kobe said a little impatiently. "It's six o'clock, and I have been dressed for an hour. Now do get up so I can tell you what I have planned."

Keiko sat up with a shiver. She stood up on the bunk and looked out the porthole. The ocean was dark and the sky still held no promise of the sun. A single star blinked far off on the horizon and America seemed a million miles away. Keiko glanced at Auntie Kobe and saw that she was busy saying her prayers. She slid back into bed to soak up just a few more minutes of its warmth, but Auntie Kobe saw her from the corner of her eye.

"Kei-chan," she said in the same warning

tone Mother used when she caught her doing the same thing on a school day. Keiko pulled the covers up to her nose and pretended to be asleep.

"I was going to tell you of my plan for Tama," Auntie Kobe began, "but, of course, if you would rather sleep . . ."

Keiko sprang out of bed before Auntie Kobe could say another word. "I'm up, Auntie Kobe. I want to hear," she pleaded. "I'm awake now. Tell me!"

"I have decided we must be bold," Auntie Kobe said with a sly smile. "We won't try to hide Tama at all. You will simply carry her off the ship right under everyone's nose."

Keiko tried to shake the sleep from her head. "Who? Me?" she asked. And then, just to make sure, she asked again. "Me?"

"Of course, you!" Auntie Kobe said matter-of-factly. "What could be more natural than a child carrying a cat. No one will notice at all."

"But suppose someone catches me?" she asked doubtfully. "What will I say?"

Auntie Kobe had one simple answer to all difficult questions. It was all a matter of her insides and her bones. "I just know it will work out, Kei-chan," she said cheerfully. "I have a feeling deep down inside that it will. Now don't worry."

And then, in almost the same breath, she asked Keiko if she would like to have Tama to keep for her own. "I have been thinking about it for several days now," she explained.

This time Keiko was sure she was still asleep. All her life she'd wanted a cat of her own, but Mother had always said she had enough to do taking care of four children and a flower shop without having a cat to worry about. And now, here was Auntie Kobe offering to give Tama to her just as calmly as though she were offering her a bag of beans.

"You see," she went on, "I shall be staying with my friend Mrs. Fuji, and I shall be dreadfully busy looking for Jiro. If you would like to have Tama, I do believe she might be happier living with you. I know you love her as much as I do."

Keiko just sat there grinning and swinging her legs, not knowing what to say or do. She never could find words when she was too excited or happy. Mother knew this, and so did Grandmother, and maybe even Hiro, but, of course, Auntie Kobe had no way of knowing.

She looked at Keiko and waited for her to say something.

"I'll take the very best care of her!" Keiko said enthusiastically. "And I'll carry her off the ship today just the way you want me to." If Tama were going to be her very own cat, that was all the more reason why she couldn't let her get locked up in quarantine.

By the time Keiko and Auntie Kobe finished breakfast and went up to the bridge, it was bustling with officers, all of them wearing their dress uniforms with gold buttons and braid. They had shaved and slicked down their hair and polished their shoes. They reminded Keiko of starched clothes strung out on bamboo poles, all stiff and crisp and clean. Somehow, there was a different air about the whole ship that morning, as though someone had tightened all the screws and pulled everything up taut and neat. It was like the feeling at home on New Year's when everything was fresh and clean and even the paper on the sliding *shoji* doors was new. Keiko was glad she had put on her new dress and given her hair an extra good brushing. She looked toward the west now, and already she could see a gray slip of land far off on the horizon. That's America, she told herself. And that's where I will live for a whole year with Aunt Emi and Uncle Henry. And Tama, she added quickly.

As land grew closer and loomed larger, the purser took her out on deck and showed her how the albatross had left the ship and gone back to their ocean home. "We'll be seeing American gulls soon," he said. And in a short while, he pointed to a white blur on the water. "There he comes," he called. "That's the pilot."

Keiko and Auntie Kobe watched as the pilot boat drew closer and closer and finally nosed its way alongside the *Nikko Maru*. Keiko held her breath as she watched the pilot climb up the wiggly rope ladder.

"We're in good hands now," the captain said as he shook the pilot's hand. Now it was the pilot who guided the ship safely through the Golden Gate, under the bright orange bridge that spanned it, and into San Francisco Bay. As they neared Alcatraz Island with its lonely prison, another boat came to meet them, and this time it was the quarantine officer— the horrible man who might take Tama away from her. Keiko felt nervous, but Auntie Kobe was calm. "Tama is safe," she whispered. "Don't you worry."

Then Keiko saw another bridge stretching across the bay, and there was San Francisco at one end of it, its hundreds of buildings rising in the sunny haze toward the sky. They clustered together as though to keep warm, and they covered the hills like a jagged white carpet. For a moment Keiko felt a small thrust of disappointment. Somehow, she had expected the buildings to glisten and glitter, but there wasn't one that was made of silver or gold.

A small red tug eased the *Nikko Maru* into her berth, and soon Keiko could see many people moving about on the pier below. Then, suddenly, she saw them!

"There they are!" she shouted. "There's Aunt Emi and Uncle Henry." She pointed them out so that Auntie Kobe and the purser could see. They looked just about as Keiko thought they would, except, naturally, they were not in their wedding finery. Aunt Emi wore a navy-blue hat and coat and Uncle Henry wore a gray top coat. When they saw Keiko, Aunt Emi waved a white handkerchief and Uncle Henry took off his hat and waved it back and forth.

"*Mah,* they look nice," Auntie Kobe said, and

the knot of worry inside Keiko eased just a little.

Before they could come on board, however, the customs inspector and the company agent and all sorts of important-looking people hurried up the gangplank. They sat at the table in the dining salon like a row of solemn-faced judges, and soon the table was covered with folders and papers and questionnaires. The purser sat in the midst of it all, reporting on the cargo and answering questions while the officers smoked cigars and stamped passports and papers. Finally, the quarantine officer asked about animals.

"Well, there are the parakeets in the captain's quarters and the tropical fish in my cabin and the chief engineer's," the purser said quietly. Keiko held her breath. Would he tell now, she wondered? But he said nothing about a black cat in Auntie Kobe's cabin, and his face was calm and serene.

Keiko decided she couldn't take any more chances. She'd get Tama off the ship right now while everyone was busy shuffling and stamping all those papers. If she could just get off and give her to Aunt Emi, everything would be fine. Keiko slipped quietly toward the door and then dashed down the corridor, running on tiptoe so no one would hear. She turned the corner like a gust of wind, and bang, she ran smack into two people who turned out to be Aunt Emi and Uncle Henry themselves! What a fine dignified meeting that was, Keiko thought, and she forgot all about the polite bow she was going to make.

Aunt Emi gathered her in her arms anyway. "How like your mother you look," she said.

But Keiko thought it was Aunt Emi who looked like Mother. She had the same quick smile and was just as small and slim—only her hair was shorter and her eyes didn't have the lonely, tired look Mother's often had.

Uncle Henry thrust his hand toward Keiko and shook hers so hard that it hurt. "Welcome to California," he said in a loud voice, and then he added, "Let's get your bags and be off." Keiko could see that he was the kind of man who got right down to business and didn't waste a minute.

"I have something else . . ." Keiko began as Uncle Henry prepared to go. "It's a sort of . . . friend." Until then, she hadn't even thought how she would tell them about Tama.

But at that very moment, Auntie Kobe herself burst into the cabin with Tama in her arms. "Here, Kei-chan," she said breathlessly. "Take her quickly before anyone comes." And only after she had thrust Tama into Keiko's arms did she bow and greet her aunt and uncle.

"How very nice to meet you," she said calmly, as though she were quite used to bursting into people's rooms with cats to give away.

Keiko quickly explained about Auntie Kobe and Jiro and Tama, and about how they had hidden Tama under the bunk. The words came all in a sudden rush and left Aunt Emi and Uncle Henry with strange, puzzled looks on their faces.

"I believe the cat should be held in quarantine, shouldn't she?" Uncle Henry said with a frown. "There are regulations about bringing in animals from another country."

Keiko's heart sank. After all that hiding and planning, here was her very own uncle talking about putting Tama in quarantine. "But you can't, Uncle Henry," she burst out. "You just can't report Tama. They'll do terrible things to her."

"Nonsense," Uncle Henry said briskly. "It's all routine. And did you say you were going to bring the cat home with you?"

Keiko could tell by the way he kept calling Tama the cat, that Uncle Henry didn't like cats at all.

Aunt Emi spoke quickly. "It's just that we've never had pets before because of the plants," she explained. "The stray cats have broken so many cuttings and even had kittens on the sterilized sand."

"There are the gold fish too," Uncle Henry added.

Everyone became silent and embarrassed then, and Keiko looked down at her toes. What was going to happen now?

And then just to make everything even worse, the quarantine officer himself stepped into the cabin. Keiko knew then and there that she might just as well give up. She shoved Tama toward the officer. "Here," she said dismally.

The officer took Tama and looked her over. "Nice cat," he said briskly. He examined her fur and looked into her mouth and peered into her eyes. "Yup," he said, "a very nice cat." And he handed Tama back to Keiko.

"But aren't you going to keep her?" she asked.

"Doesn't she have to be held in quarantine?" Uncle Henry wondered.

The officer shook his head. "Nope," he answered. "As long as she's healthy, we don't want her. She's all yours." And he left the cabin as quickly as he'd come.

Now there was only Uncle Henry. "I'll make sure she doesn't get into any trouble," Keiko said hopefully.

"She's really a very well-behaved cat," Auntie Kobe added.

She was so relieved Tama wasn't being taken to quarantine that she had to sit down and wipe her face with a handkerchief. "*Mah*, I'm glad Tama is safe," she sighed.

"Oh, do let's try keeping her," Aunt Emi coaxed. "I'm sure it will work out."

And finally Uncle Henry agreed. "Very well then," he said reluctantly, "but if she gets into trouble . . ." He didn't finish the sentence, but he didn't need to. Keiko knew exactly what he meant.

It wasn't fun at all to say good-by again. Auntie Kobe left with her friend, Mrs. Fuji, saying she would phone Keiko soon. The ship's officers came to stand at the head of the gangplank, and each one shook Keiko's hand as she left.

"Be a good girl," the purser said at the very last. "And take good care of your cat," he added.

"I trust she had an enjoyable trip across the Pacific," the captain whispered in her ear. He chuckled as he gave Tama a friendly pat on the head, and Keiko began to wonder if she and

Auntie Kobe had really had a secret after all.

"I'll see you next year when I go home," Keiko called back brightly as she waved to them from the pier. The officers smiled and waved back, but when Keiko saw the look on Aunt Emi's face, she knew she had said the wrong thing. She had scarcely set foot on America and already she was talking of going home. Keiko sighed and held Tama close, but even Tama seemed to know things weren't quite right. "Eeeeooooowwwwrrrr," she said mournfully, making Uncle Henry turn around and give her a dismal look.

5

The First Worry

Keiko could tell when they reached Uncle Henry's house, for as they turned onto Forty-seventh Street from the road that led off the freeway, she could see a white frame house with rows and rows of greenhouses stretched out behind it. Those would be for all the carnations Uncle Henry grew. Keiko knew he was one of the best carnation growers in all of Richmond, for Mother had told her about the prizes his flowers had won at the County Fair. The greenhouses sat in the sun, as if to hoard its warmth so that the plants inside would grow strong and tall. Keiko looked at all the glass panes, spattered with paint so that the sun wouldn't be too strong, and told herself she would have to be careful if she ever got hold of a ball and bat. She had broken one window when Hiro let her use his, and after that, he had never let her touch them again. "You aren't ready to learn," he had said flatly, and that was the end of that.

Aunt Emi led the way up the steps and opened the door to let Keiko step inside first. "Well, Kei-chan, here is your new home," she said. "I do hope you will like it."

Keiko kicked off her shoes just as she did at home, not remembering to put them neatly together as she stepped into the house.

"You don't have to do that here," Aunt Emi reminded her, smiling. Still Keiko didn't feel right walking all over the beautiful gray rug with her dirty shoes, and she moved around the room on tiptoe. There was a wonderful, soft-looking couch with a gay flowered cover, and in front of it was a low coffee table with a bowl of tiny red chrysanthemums. Over in the corner was a television set with a square of silk thrown over it, and on the wall beside it hung a beautiful old scroll with a black-ink painting of an eagle. There was a fireplace of yellow brick, and on the mantel above it were a potted dwarf pine and a Japanese doll that danced forever inside a glass case. She looked just like one they had at home, and Aunt Emi explained how Keiko's grandmother had given one to Aunt Emi and one to Keiko's mother when they were both young girls.

"They belonged to Grandmother once,"

Aunt Emi explained. She grew silent a moment as the past crowded about her with dozens of memories, but she soon sighed and hurried Keiko on. "Come along and see your room," she urged.

They went on through the dining room and the sunny kitchen and into the room Aunt Emi had fixed up for Keiko. "There now," she said proudly, and she stepped back for Keiko to see. "Do you like it?"

Keiko couldn't say a word. She just stared at the maple bed with the matching dresser and the desk, where she could study, and the bookcase waiting to be filled with books. She saw the sun coming in through the pale lemon-colored curtains at the window, making the bright quilt on her bed look like a beautiful crazy design inside a kaleidoscope. She looked outside beyond the greenhouses and saw the low green hills dotted with houses. It was a lovely room. It was the kind of room Keiko couldn't even begin to dream about back home.

"Do you like it?" Aunt Emi asked again.

Keiko tried to think of the most beautiful thing she had ever seen to compare it to, but she had never seen anything quite so nice. "It's

. . . it's prettier than the Emperor's palace!" she said finally, even though she had no more idea what that was like than the inside of the moon.

"I'm going to like it here, Aunt Emi," Keiko added. "I know I am."

The anxious look fell away from Aunt Emi's face, and she kissed Keiko on the cheek. "I'm so glad," she said, smiling. "I can't tell you how much."

Uncle Henry came in with her bags and put them down beside her bed. "I put a box in the laundry for your cat," he said. "Come along and I'll show it to you."

Keiko had been so excited, she'd almost forgotten till now that she was clutching Tama in her arms. Keiko had planned to put a warm soft piece of wool inside a cardboard carton and put it at the foot of her bed for Tama. But Uncle Henry seemed to have another idea altogether. He led the way to the laundry and pointed to a cardboard carton in which he had laid an old burlap sack. He put it under the laundry tubs, squeezed in between one of the tub legs and the great U-curve of the drainpipe.

"Think this'll do?" he asked Keiko.

It was horrible, but Keiko didn't dare say a

word. She bent down to put Tama in her bed and tried to sound pleased. "There, Tama," she said. "This is your nice new bed."

But Tama wasn't fooled for a moment. She seemed to know this was nothing more than an old carton squeezed next to a dirty old drainpipe. She leaped quickly out of the box, flicked her tail, and stalked out of the room like an angry duchess.

"I guess she's tired of living in cartons," Keiko said helplessly.

But Uncle Henry just shrugged. "That's all I have to offer," he said, and if the doorbell hadn't rung just then, Keiko wouldn't have known what to do. She was all out of words again.

Uncle Henry went to the door, and there was the first of a stream of friends who had come to call.

"So your niece has arrived safely," they said, bowing and smiling. "How nice to have a new daughter in your home."

They brought platters of vinegared rice balls garnished with shrimp and tuna; they brought sweet bean-paste cakes and chocolate layer cake, and quarts of strawberry and butter-brickle ice cream. They congratulated Aunt

Emi and Uncle Henry, and they told Keiko what a lovely little girl she was. For a while, Keiko bowed and smiled and said thank you, as though it were New Year's Day and she had left all her wickedness behind in the year just past. But before very long, she discovered it wasn't much fun sitting among a group of adults, looking like a festival doll with her hands folded on her lap and a smile curved forever on her lips. It wasn't fun at all even after she'd eaten a big dish of creamy butter-brickle ice cream.

When the food was eaten and the grownups lingered over cups of green tea, Keiko could sit still no longer. Even Tama, who had been rubbing against her legs, deserted her as though she had had quite enough of all the chatter. Keiko was filled with such a longing to be outdoors, she suddenly found herself slipping out of her chair. She didn't even ask Aunt Emi or excuse herself from all the tea-drinking ladies. She fled past the men who talked in a smoky circle in the living room and ran lightly down the front steps wondering where to start.

First she circled the pond and inspected Uncle Henry's precious gold fish and carp. "Tama would never hurt you," she called, and she tossed in a pebble to watch its ripples circle out over the surface of the water. She went on past the chrysanthemum bed and almost fell right into it head first when she bent down to smell the biggest bronze blossom. She thought how pleased Mother would be if she had some like that in her shop. Then she hurried on to the nearest greenhouse. She'd never been inside one before, and she peered in through the paint-spotted pane at the rows and rows of carnations planted in raised beds of soil and sand. As she looked, she suddenly saw a face looking back at her. It was a boy with eyes as blue as a September sky and hair the color of rice straw drying in the sun. He couldn't have been much older than she, and for a minute they stared silently at each other. Then the boy grinned and beckoned to her to come in.

Keiko could smell the moist earth and feel the warmth of the air as she stepped inside. The boy was hidden behind the bench of tall carnation plants that grew higher than his head, but Keiko heard him call.

"Hey, are you Keiko?" he asked. He seemed to know who she was without even asking.

Keiko nodded. "Who are you?" she asked.

"Mike Michaelson," the boy answered. "It's really Michael Michaelson. That's how it is on my birth certificate." And then he added, "My mother grades and packs flowers for your uncle."

"Oh," Keiko said, wondering how it would feel to have a name like Keiko Keikoson.

She wasn't at all sure what Mike was doing in the greenhouse. He seemed to move about in a most businesslike way, as though he were doing something enormously important. But when she watched closely, it seemed he was pinching all the buds off the plants.

"What are you doing anyway?" Keiko asked.

"Disbudding," Mike answered importantly.

"Oh." Keiko watched Mike for a few more minutes and then said, "If you take off all the buds, how will the flowers bloom?" Actually, it seemed a very stupid thing to be picking off the buds when you wanted them to turn into carnations some day.

Mike put his hands on his hips and looked at Keiko through a piece of hair that fell over his eyes.

"You don't know much about carnation growing, do you?" he asked.

He looked at Keiko in exactly the same way

Hiro did when he was doing something Keiko didn't know how to do. It was the look Hiro gave her when Mother let him help with the accounts, for instance. He would use the abacus and write neat black figures in the ledger with his fountain pen and act as though he were the only one in the whole house who knew anything at all.

Keiko was about to tell Mike she had come from Japan only this morning and how could she possibly know anything about carnation growing, when he spoke again.

"If you don't pinch off the small buds on the side, you don't get a big flower in the middle," he explained. "See?"

And all Keiko could say again was, "Oh."

Mike went back to work again, looking very serious, studying each plant carefully to pinch off just the small tight buds that wedged themselves in close to the main bud. Keiko could feel her fingers twitching for wanting to try it herself, but Mike didn't say anything about letting her help. Keiko decided to wait until Mike got busy and then go around to another bench and try pinching a few buds herself. It was easy to slip away, for Mike didn't seem to have much more to say to her. Keiko had just found a spot Mike hadn't already worked on and broken off a few tiny green buds with her nails, when she heard the door open and saw Uncle Henry come in. Mike saw him too, and for a minute he looked as though he wanted to sink right through the dirt floor.

"Well, Mike," Uncle Henry said. "What are you doing?"

Keiko liked the way Mike admitted right off that he had been disbudding when he could have just said he was looking around. She felt as though she ought to be on his side and she spoke up quickly.

"I helped him too," she said, "just a little bit."

Uncle Henry frowned and spoke slowly, as though he were choosing each word very carefully from a file stored away in the back of his head. "We have a rule here, Keiko, that children are not to do any work in the greenhouses unless an adult is there to supervise. The work may look simple, but there are correct ways to do everything, and if you don't know the right way, you can do more harm than good."

Keiko nodded.

"I was only trying to help," Mike said lamely. "Mom said you were shorthanded."

"Thank you, Mike," Uncle Henry said stiffly, "but from now on, just give me help when I ask for it, will you?"

Keiko watched as Mike nodded and dug his toe into the dirt. And even when Uncle Henry tried to make everything all right again by showing them the new cuttings in the fresh clean sand, she still felt annoyed with him. He didn't like cats and he hadn't been at all nice to Mike Michaelson. Uncle Henry explained how the cuttings were kept warm and watered every minute by an automatic sprinkler and how they took root in just six weeks with this new system. But Keiko couldn't feel interested at all. After a while, when she saw Mike slip outside, she went outside too, leaving Uncle Henry in his greenhouse to inspect the cuttings all by himself.

It wasn't until that night that Uncle Henry began to sneeze. He sneezed and sneezed and then he began to sniffle, until Aunt Emi was sure he had caught cold. By the time Keiko was ready for bed, Uncle Henry's eyes were red-rimmed and bleary and he said his throat felt scratchy. He was still sneezing when Keiko said good night and went to bed in her lovely pale yellow room. Aunt Emi came to tuck her in and Keiko lay in her brand-new bed, her eyes wide open and staring into the darkness because she wanted to think. She would have to be careful not to roll around too much, for being in bed was another matter entirely from sleeping on the floor where you couldn't fall more than an inch no matter how much you tossed. Keiko lay stiff and straight, her arms at her sides, as she had learned to do in the bunk on the *Nikko Maru*. And then she thought about all the things that had happened since morning. This was something she liked to do even when she was at home, especially if there had been something exciting during the day, like the time a man had stolen the milk right out of the milk box at their gate and Hiro had chased him clear down to the station before he got away.

Keiko thought now about Uncle Henry and how he hadn't wanted Tama to come home with her at all. She wondered how poor Tama was, all alone in that cold, dark laundry. She remembered the stern look on Uncle Henry's face when he talked to her and Mike in the greenhouse, and she began to wonder if she wanted to stay even a year. After all, Mother had said she could come home whenever she pleased. Maybe she would just skip trying to be a good daughter to anybody. She wished she were asleep on her own quilt next to Grandmother and Hana right this minute. She wished she could hear Mother singing to Kenbo to make him go to sleep. She would have been happy even to hear Hiro grumble about somebody having touched his precious bug collection. Suddenly, everybody at home seemed so far away. Keiko felt hot tears trickle down her cheeks and plop on the pillow one by one. It hadn't been a good thing at all to come to America to live.

Keiko turned over onto her stomach and then discovered that if she breathed very softly, she could hear Uncle Henry and Aunt Emi talking in the kitchen.

"Of course it must be the cat," Uncle Henry was saying. "I'm sure I'm allergic to cat hair. I remember how I used to sneeze in Osaka when we had that big yellow cat."

Aunt Emi's voice was worried and thin. "But Papa-san," she said anxiously, "we just can't ask Kei-chan to give Tama up now. She's so fond of her and she will be lonely until she is used to us."

Keiko could hear Uncle Henry sigh. "I know . . . I know . . ." he said slowly. "Well, I guess . . ." and then he sneezed an enormous sneeze and got up from his chair. Keiko never did hear the rest of his sentence. He guessed . . . what? Keiko would never know.

Keiko curled up into a tight ball now and worked up a big worry. How would she ever get Uncle Henry to like Tama if she made him sniffle and sneeze? Keiko knew this was a problem only Auntie Kobe with her deep feelings would be able to cope with. She would call her up first thing in the morning, and maybe she'd have a feeling in her bones about just the right thing to do.

6

Too Many Cats

Keiko hurried from her room the next morning and discovered that Uncle Henry had already eaten and gone to take a shipment of flowers to the airport.

"I've been waiting for you," Aunt Emi said cheerfully, and she took a pan of piping-hot golden-brown biscuits from the oven.

"Now, have some orange juice," she urged, "and I'll make you some bacon and eggs. I do want you to start off your second day in America with a good breakfast."

She bustled back and forth between the big white refrigerator and the table, bringing out butter and honey and strawberry jam and cream, spreading everything out in front of Keiko at the table. Keiko knew she could love Aunt Emi without any trouble at all, but Uncle Henry was another matter entirely.

Keiko hurried to the laundry for just a quick look to see if Tama was all right, but when she looked in, the carton was empty. "Where's

Tama?" she asked, and quickly she checked the other rooms. "I don't see Tama anywhere," she said to her aunt.

Aunt Emi slipped a plate of sizzling bacon and a sunny-side-up egg in front of her and told her to hurry and eat before everything got cold. When she saw that Keiko had begun to eat, she explained, "Uncle Henry thought Tama would be happier outside last night, so he let her out. I'm sure she'll be home as soon as she gets hungry."

Keiko agreed that she thought she would, and for a while, until she had eaten three biscuits dripping with butter and honey, she didn't feel worried at all about Tama. She licked the sticky sweetness from around her mouth, and when Aunt Emi wasn't looking, she even licked the honey that had stuck to her knife. But before long, Keiko began to wonder just how long cats stayed away before they came home for breakfast.

"Aunt Emi," she said, "do you think Tama might like some dried fish?"

Aunt Emi nodded. "I think she might at that," she answered. "I'll get you some I bought from Mr. Ito's grocery truck just last week." And then she saw how worried Keiko was and suggested she take the fish out on the back porch. "You just sit on the steps with those dried mackerel for a while," she said, laughing, "and you'll probably have every cat in the neighborhood, as well as Tama, coming to beg for some."

As Keiko started outside, Aunt Emi called after her, "Don't go off too far now. As soon as your uncle gets back from the airport, we're going to San Francisco."

"I won't," Keiko answered, but it was the kind of proper answer she could give without having listened at all to what came before it. She was very good at that because Grandmother was always telling her to watch out for Kenbo or to come home before it got dark or to wash her hands before she ate, and Keiko always managed to give the right answer even though she had only half heard what Grandmother said.

Clutching her dried fish in one hand now, Keiko started down the back steps and out toward the greenhouses. Surely Tama must be somewhere nearby. Keiko went to the shed where Uncle Henry kept his rotor tiller and his tractor and his flower pots and sacks of fertilizer.

"Tama," she called into the shadowy stillness, but nothing moved except a butterfly that struggled up toward the sky.

Next Keiko went up and down between the greenhouses. She climbed over old coils of hose and wire, over broken pots and panes of glass and old boxes turned upside down. She looked into every clump of weed, peered behind corners, and even looked up at the sun-warmed glass roofs where a cat might like to take a little nap.

"Tama, where are you?" she called until she was hoarse, but no black cat came bounding up to meet her. Keiko was soon past the last greenhouse, near the underpass beneath the freeway with its whizzing cars. She thought for one horrible moment what might have happened if Tama had somehow wandered up onto the freeway, but she brushed such a terrible idea aside as quickly as a cobweb. She turned at the last greenhouse and walked down the sidewalk that skirted Uncle Henry's property. It was all his fault for letting Tama out in the first place, she thought crossly, and for being allergic to Tama and giving her such a horrible bed. Keiko kicked at a stone and sent it flying down the sidewalk. When she looked up, she saw that she had almost hit Mike. He was riding an old black bike with his head held high, whistling "Yankee Doodle," and looking as though he owned the whole world. Behind him a big old hound loped along, his tail wagging, his tongue hanging out. Mike slowed down when he saw Keiko.

"Hey," he called. "What's the matter?"

"Tama's lost," Keiko said miserably. "What will I tell Auntie Kobe?"

Mike scratched his head. "Who're Tama and Auntie Kobe? And what're you carrying around that smelly fish for?" He held his nose and made a face. "P-U!" he said.

Keiko quickly hid the fish behind her back and then told Mike about Auntie Kobe and Jiro and about how they had hidden Tama on the ship all the way across the Pacific and how she belonged to her now, except that she was lost.

Mike straddled his bike, his dirty gray sneakers planted firmly on the sidewalk, his arms crossed over his chest. "How about that!" he said, looking impressed. "I lost a dog once."

"Did you find him?" Keiko asked.

Mike shook his head. "Nope, but Pop got

King Arthur for me over at the Humane Society." Mike reached out to give King Arthur a pat on the head. "Hey, I'll bet somebody found Tama and took her to the Humane Society," he said suddenly. "That's where she is, I'll bet."

Mike's enthusiasm was catching. "Do you think so?" Keiko asked. "Do you really?"

Mike was positive now. "Sure. I'll bet you anything that's where she is right now, chewing on a big fat old fishbone." He held his nose again and said, "Phew-cce! Even a cat wouldn't want that smelly ol' fish."

Keiko tried not to mind what Mike was saying about her dried fish. "Will you take me to the Humane Society to look for her?" she asked.

Mike backed away. "Who, me?" he asked. "Heck, no!"

"I could ride on the back of your bike," Keiko suggested. "I'm not very heavy."

Mike kept backing away inch by inch. "Me ride a girl on my bike?" he asked. "You're crazy!"

Keiko stood there feeling sorry for herself. "I'll never find Tama then," she said forlornly. "I'll probably never have another cat again in my whole entire life."

Keiko made Mike feel just bad enough to offer to go to the Humane Society himself. It was Saturday, and he really didn't have anything special to do until time for his paper route. "Aw, I'll go then," he said at last. "But I'm going by myself. I'll go look for your ol' black cat."

"With yellow eyes and white paws and white on the tip of her tail," Keiko called after him. But Mike was already on his way. He was riding no hands now, and he whistled as he rode away.

Keiko felt better and ran the rest of the way home. When she got there, she saw Aunt Emi standing on the porch, looking worried.

"Oh, there you are, Kei-chan," she said. "I was beginning to worry about you. Do hurry. Auntie Kobe is going to San Francisco with us."

Keiko felt her heart flip over. "Did you tell her Tama was lost?" she asked.

"No, no, of course not," Aunt Emi said quickly. "Besides, I don't think she's lost at all. We'll leave a saucer of milk for her on the porch, and she'll probably be sitting there by the time we get back."

If she isn't, Mike will find her for me at the

Humane Society, Keiko thought. But just to be on the safe side, Keiko took her dried fish out onto the porch and tied it to the railing with a piece of old string.

Then they got into Uncle Henry's car. Aunt Emi got in back and Keiko sat up in front because Aunt Emi said maybe Keiko could see more that way, and she'd sit in back and keep Auntie Kobe company. Keiko sat up straight and still, looking out the window to the right and only glancing at Uncle Henry out of the corner of her eye from time to time. As they drove toward Oakland to get Auntie Kobe, Keiko could tell that Uncle Henry felt better today. For one thing, he had stopped sneezing, and for another, he had just sent a good shipment of carnations to the wholesaler in Chicago.

"They may double their Christmas order from us this year," he said, speaking of the wholesaler now. Keiko looked at him to show that she had heard, but Uncle Henry kept his eyes on the road and looked straight ahead. "If they keep expanding, they may double their orders for the rest of the year as well."

Aunt Emi sounded pleased. "How wonderful!" she said. "Maybe we'll be able to get that new automatic washer after all. And we'll start a college fund for you, Kei-chan, and get you some new books and clothes for school. You'll be going when the new term begins in February . . ." She was full of ideas, and it was hard for Keiko to be silent and sulk over Tama when Aunt Emi was so nice.

"Look," her aunt said now, pointing first to the right and then to the left as they drove through Oakland. "There's Lake Merritt, and that's the city hall over there, and the court house, and the library . . ."

Even Uncle Henry added words between Aunt Emi's as he pointed out the duck feeding station and the playground and the boathouse, where you could rent row boats to take out on the lake.

And then they were in front of Mrs. Fuji's gray house with its cracked and peeling paint, and Auntie Kobe came hurrying into the car, filling it with her talk and cheerful laugh.

She was so busy talking about the enormous baked ham Mrs. Fuji had made the night before that, much to Keiko's relief, she seemed to have forgotten all about Tama and didn't even ask how she was. And when she'd finished with the ham, she talked of Jiro and how she had dreamed of him last night and how she had such a strong feeling that he was very near.

As Uncle Henry sped over the silver bridge that spanned the bay, Keiko closed her eyes against the glint of the sun on the water and tried hard to see if she couldn't have a feeling too—only about Tama. But all she saw were bright red and yellow spots flickering before her closed lids and the only feeling she had was the gurgle in her stomach. Keiko decided she just wasn't very good about having deep feelings about anything yet.

And it wasn't long before even Keiko herself stopped thinking about Tama, for now there was just too much to see all around. Uncle Henry took them first to Golden Gate Park, which turned out to be the biggest, greenest park Keiko had ever seen. It went on and on for what seemed like miles, and it even had an aquarium full of strange fish and a tea garden that looked like a garden in Kyoto. Keiko climbed the steep drum bridge and made a wish as she looked down into the pond, and she sat at the top of the stone steps that led to a temple gate and thought about the day her class had gone to Nikko for its spring excursion. Someone had gone off with her shoes from the hundreds of pairs lined up outside the shrine, and when she'd come out and not been able to find hers, her teacher, Miss Kawai, had gone to one of the souvenir shops and bought her a pair of wooden clogs. They were beautiful, with red velveteen thongs. Mother had sent some money with Keiko the very next day to pay for them, but Miss Kawai had said no, she wanted to give them to Keiko as a present. Keiko had never had a present from a teacher before, and she put the clogs away in a special box and never wanted to use them so they would last forever. She knew even now just where she had left them in her closet, warning Hana that she must never, never borrow them. Keiko sat there thinking about Miss Kawai and Nikko and Mother and Hiro and Hana and everybody back home when Aunt Emi called her.

"Come along, Kei-chan," she said. "There's lots more to see in San Francisco," and she came over and took her hand, just as Mother used to do when she was a little girl.

They went next to see the sea lions stretched out on the big brown ocean-sprayed rock near the Cliff House. Keiko could smell again the familiar salt spray of the ocean, and Auntie Kobe began to talk about the *Nikko Maru* and Captain Sawada and the night of the *sukiyaki* party when she had fainted.

"*Mah,* but those officers were all nice," Auntie Kobe said. "I almost wish I were back on that beautiful green ship again."

Before Auntie Kobe could grow too homesick, Uncle Henry hurried them on to the zoo and then to Fisherman's Wharf with its fleet of crab boats and the vendors who sold crab from steaming cauldrons right out on the sidewalk. They ate in a restaurant with windows that looked out over the wharf, and it was only when Keiko saw a plate of broiled trout go by that she thought of Tama and wondered if by now she were back nibbling at the fish on the railing. And then, as though Auntie Kobe could read her mind, she suddenly turned and asked Keiko how Tama was getting along.

Keiko wanted to crawl right under the table. She just couldn't bear to tell Auntie Kobe she had lost her beautiful Tama on the very first day she'd had her. And then Aunt Emi came to her rescue.

"Why, Tama's fine," she said brightly. "She's

been out exploring the neighborhood, and by now she's probably found some fine new friends."

Auntie Kobe smiled and looked pleased. "I just knew Tama would be happy living with Kei-chan," she said. "I knew I had decided to do the right thing."

Keiko looked down at her lap and twisted her napkin. Aunt Emi coughed gently, and Uncle Henry sneezed as though the very thought of Tama were too much for him. Only Auntie Kobe went right on eating her fresh crab as though she hadn't a worry in the world.

When it was time to go home, they took the ferry back to the Oakland pier, and Keiko went all over the ship looking into people's faces to see if she might not find a Japanese man, about forty, with a scar down his cheek. She would feel a little better about having lost Tama if she could make up for it by finding Jiro. But even though Auntie Kobe had felt that Jiro was very close, he wasn't so close that he was on the same ferryboat.

They took Auntie Kobe back to Mrs. Fuji's peeling gray house, and when they got back home to Richmond, there was Mike sitting on the front steps waiting for them. He held an

enormous cardboard carton on his lap, and he
was reading a comic book. Keiko took one look
at the carton and raced out of the car. "Mike,
you found her!" she shouted.

"Wait'll you see what I found," Mike said,
getting to his feet.

Aunt Emi invited him inside. "What in the
world have you got in that carton?" she asked.
"It looks so heavy."

"Yes, ma'am," Mike puffed. "It *is* heavy."
And picking it up with a great deal of effort,
he started inside.

"Wait a minute," Uncle Henry called. "I'll
give you a hand."

But Mike had already staggered into the
house with his carton, and just as he got inside, he tripped on the rug and fell sprawling
to the floor. As he fell, he dropped his box,
the flaps flew open, and from inside jumped
not one black cat, but three! They leaped out
with frightened yowls and then proceeded to
run in different directions all over the house.

"Stop!" Keiko shouted, but the cats spread
like black ink. One ran into the bedroom and
hid under the bed; the second ran into the
kitchen and leaped to the top of the china cabinet; the third scrambled up the drapes in the

living room and perched on the curtain rod, glaring at everybody like a small black panther.

"I couldn't tell which was Tama," Mike explained hopelessly, "so I brought all three of them back." He reached into his pocket and pulled out a turtle with its back painted yellow. "I got me a turtle, too," he said proudly, but Aunt Emi asked him to please put it away and help catch the cats.

Keiko ran into the kitchen first and stared

up at the cat on the cabinet. "You're not Tama at all," she said dismally, "but you'd better come down anyway."

The cat just looked at her with its yellow-green eyes and twitched its black tail. Keiko got up on a chair, reached up toward the cat, and knocked Uncle Henry's coffee cup into the sink with a crash. Now Mike chased the second cat into the kitchen too, where it ran under the stove and glared at him like a black witch. "Hissssss," it said wickedly.

"Darned cat!" Mike muttered, and he dived under the stove, grabbed the struggling cat, and shouted, "Hey, if this isn't Tama, open the door. Quick!"

It wasn't Tama and Keiko opened the door.

"Darn ol' cat," Mike muttered again, and he watched as it leaped away down the steps.

Aunt Emi hurried into the kitchen with a broom, which she shook at the cat up on the cabinet. "Come down this instant," she demanded, and she waved the broom in the cat's face until it leaped onto the table, where Mike caught it at last.

"Out you go too," he said, and he shooed it out the back door.

Now there was only the cat sitting on the

curtain rod in the living room. Uncle Henry glared at it as he moved all the breakable things from the tables nearby.

"I'll make her move," Mike said, and leaping and clapping his hands at the cat, he shouted, "Scat!"

The cat moved, all right. It landed right on the mantel and crouched beside the dancing doll in the glass case.

"Oh, don't let her break that," Aunt Emi said frantically. "Somebody do something!"

While the cat glared at Mike, Uncle Henry tiptoed quietly from behind, made a quick snatch, and finally got the screeching, scratching cat out of the house. By the time he closed the door, he was rubbing his eyes and sneezing again.

"I'll be glad if I never see another cat in this house again," he said gloomily, and he blew his nose and marched out of the room.

"All that trouble for nothing," Mike said miserably.

"And Uncle Henry still hates cats," Keiko added dismally.

She sighed and went out to look at the back porch. The milk was still in the saucer and the fish hung limply on the railing. They were right back where they had started in the morning, except that now Mike had a pet turtle.

"I'm going to call him Herbert," he said, "after my shop teacher." And he put it in his pocket and went home.

7

Smog and a Feeling

Bed was really a fine place for worrying, and Keiko worried about all sorts of things after she got in hers. In the first place it was quiet and warm and dark there. You could lie with your knees scrunched up to your chest, your hands clenched, and your toes curled and have a great big worry all to yourself.

"Now don't you worry about Tama," Aunt Emi said soothingly as she tucked Keiko in that night. "She'll be back soon. You wait and see."

But how could Keiko not worry? Tama was lost, Uncle Henry didn't like cats, and she couldn't tell Auntie Kobe about her problem until Tama came back. Somehow it all made Keiko feel very sad, but tonight there were no tears plopping on her pillow.

As she lay in the darkness, Keiko thought of Captain Sawada and the purser and the *Nikko Maru* sailing for Los Angeles, and like Auntie Kobe, she wished a little that she were back in the middle of the Pacific Ocean, in that floating world of *sukiyaki* parties and pink sherbet.

When she awoke, it was Sunday, and Keiko could hear church bells from somewhere. They rang high and clear with a cheerful sound, like yellow and gold and white bells glistening in the sun and not like the dark bronze bells of the temples in Tokyo that seemed to ring mostly at twilight. The sun was hidden behind a murky grayness of smoke and fog, but inside there was the delicious smell of pancakes. Keiko hurried to the kitchen.

"Good morning, Aunt Emi . . . Uncle Henry," she called. But no one was there to answer. The coffee was made, a pan of cocoa steamed on the stove, and four pancakes sizzled faintly on the griddle, waiting to be eaten.

"Aunt Emi," Keiko called again, but still no one answered. Keiko heard only the ticking of the clock on the wall, and she knew something was wrong. It was the same empty feeling that had filled the house when Father had gone to the sanitarium. Keiko ran outside and saw her uncle and aunt walking slowly toward the house, their faces solemn and grim.

"What's wrong?" Keiko called. She knew it had something to do with the carnations.

"The smog has spoiled over half the flowers we were going to ship tomorrow," Aunt Emi said dismally. "The petals of all the red and pink carnations are burned, and some of them have even begun to fold up."

Keiko remembered what Uncle Henry had told her about the chemicals and gases in the air. "Air pollution" he had called it, telling her it was worst on days when the air was still and fumes from the chemical factories nearby clung to the plants. She could tell even without a deep Auntie Kobe-like feeling that this meant trouble for Uncle Henry. "What's going to happen?" she asked anxiously.

"I take a loss on the shipment," Uncle Henry said, his forehead wrinkled with a frown. "And as if that weren't bad enough, the new cuttings are diseased and the mice have been eating the flowers again."

"They've nipped the flowers right off the stems!" Aunt Emi said indignantly. "Imagine!"

Keiko knew that if Tama were here, she could catch the mice without any trouble at all, even though Uncle Henry told her these mice were so clever that he hadn't been able to catch them with a baited trap.

Uncle Henry went to the telephone and sent a wire to the wholesaler in Chicago, telling him he could not make his regular shipment tomorrow.

"They may cancel their big Christmas order if this happens again," he said, shaking his head. "They may decide to order from the growers in Colorado instead." This was the second time in a month that he had had to cancel an order, although the last time it was because fog had grounded the planes.

Keiko knew it would be a dreadful thing if the Chicago wholesaler canceled their order. She tried to think of something cheerful to say. She told how Mother had to cancel an order for a wedding bouquet once when she got sick and couldn't open the shop. "No one was angry with her," she explained.

"But your mother's is only one small shop," Uncle Henry interrupted. "I send flowers to wholesalers who supply dozens of small shops in more than one state. When I can't ship my flowers, dozens and dozens of people are involved." He shook his head again and sighed deeply.

"If we had known the smog was coming, maybe we could have saved the flowers before they were damaged," Aunt Emi said slowly.

Uncle Henry just shrugged. "Who knows?" he said.

Keiko could think of nothing else that might cheer them up. She sipped her cocoa silently, but it had grown lukewarm and the pancakes were cold and soggy.

Finally, Aunt Emi looked up at the clock, brushed her hands as though to end the whole dismal affair, and announced she was going to church. "It's my turn to be in charge of the flowers," she explained. "Besides, we can't make anything better by sitting here and worrying. Come along, Kei-chan. I'll take you to our church school."

But going to church school was the last thing Keiko wanted to do. Suppose Tama came home and didn't find anybody to feed her or let her in! She might run off again and never come back.

Aunt Emi seemed disappointed, but she knew that finding Tama was more important for Keiko right now than anything else.

"I'll be back soon," she said as she left. "If you want anything, tell Uncle Henry, and if you get hungry, just look in the refrigerator. I'll be back in time for lunch."

As soon as she left, Uncle Henry hurried outside to start cutting the carnations that had been damaged, and Keiko was left all alone. She went to the window to see if maybe Tama might be coming down the street, flicking her tail and walking like a duchess. But the street was empty. Suddenly, the telephone rang, and when Keiko answered it, it was Auntie Kobe.

"What do you think?" she asked in a voice that trembled with excitement.

"You found Jiro-san!" Keiko said immediately.

"No, no, but I am getting close," Auntie Kobe explained. "Captain Sawada telephoned me from Los Angeles, saying he heard of a man who sounds like he might be my Jiro. And what do you think? A friend of Mrs. Fuji's is going to let me ride along in his car, and so I'm going to Los Angeles!" The words came in a breathless rush, and Keiko could barely understand what she said.

"Are you going today?" she asked.

"In half an hour," Auntie Kobe answered. "I'll write to you, Kei-chan. Be a good girl and take good care of Tama. My greetings to your aunt and uncle." And then with a little click she was gone.

Keiko put the telephone back on its cradle, flopped down on the couch, and began to feel sorry for herself. Everyone was gone. Not only Tama, but now even Auntie Kobe. She glanced around the room, wondering what to do with herself, and went over to look at the dancing doll on the mantel. She tried standing as the doll did, her head tipped to one side, one foot placed daintily behind the other, a parasol raised over her shoulder—but all she managed to do was lose her balance. Mother had tried to make her take dancing lessons once, but she had made a terrible fuss and said she would rather learn how to play baseball. The only trouble with baseball was that Hiro wouldn't teach her how, and now she could neither dance nor play baseball. It was pretty discouraging when you thought about it.

Keiko sat on the floor and thought about Hana and Hiro. It would be Monday in Tokyo, and they would probably be in school. Maybe they would be eating lunch. Keiko wondered what Mother had put in their lunch tins, and she thought of her own alumite tin with the red rose painted on top. She'd won it as a prize at school for the best composition on what she would like to be when she grew up. Most of the other girls had said they'd like to be dress designers, or teachers, or nurses, or government workers, but Keiko had said she wanted to be a scientist and discover a medicine that would cure all the sick people in the world. Then she would give it away in small blue bottles and maybe give it a long fancy name that sounded very important, like hexomyrady-calcimin—something like that. If someone had just invented a medicine like that long ago, maybe Father wouldn't have grown thin and pale and died a week before her birthday when the summer rains had come.

Mother was surprised when Keiko brought home the lunch tin. *"Mah,* such a fantastic idea!" she had said when she read Keiko's composition. But her teacher, Miss Kawai, had told her she had imagination and a soul and for her not to lose them ever. Keiko had cherished her soul ever since, although she wasn't quite sure just what it was. She knew Father would have been pleased, too, because he had often talked about people's souls and how some people in the world had souls that were fine and pure.

Keiko sat for a while thinking about Father

and about people's souls, and she wondered if Uncle Henry had one at all. If he did, Keiko thought, it couldn't be a very nice one. And yet, Aunt Emi had shown her the beautiful tea bowl he used and told her how he made better ceremonial tea than she herself.

"He'll make a cup for you someday when he doesn't have so much on his mind," she said, as she put the bowl away in its brocade bag and returned it to the shelf.

It was all very strange, because Mother had told her how one had to have a beautiful and serene mind to be a real master of the tea ceremony. Maybe Uncle Henry did have a beautiful spirit hidden somewhere inside, even though she had seen no sign of it yet.

Keiko knew that if she were really going to be a good daughter, she should go outside right now and help Uncle Henry. But somehow, she didn't want to go. Instead, she went to the kitchen and looked into the refrigerator. She opened the freezer, looked fondly at the half-gallon carton of chocolate ice cream, and took a spoonful to lick. Somehow, ice cream in the morning didn't taste quite right. It was like having Christmas in the middle of summer.

She went out to the front porch then and decided to watch for Tama or Mike.

The street was still with a Sunday quiet, and slowly the sun climbed up beyond the banks of fog. Keiko sat down on the top step and decided she would try willing Mike into coming to see her. This was something Hiro had taught her. He said if you just thought hard enough about somebody, you could make them do almost anything you willed them to do. He had told her, in fact, that he had willed Keiko into going to the store to buy sesame seed for Mother, and she had really gone. Keiko had offered to go because she wanted to see the new white puppy that had come to live at the corner store, but according to Hiro, she had gone because he had willed her to go. Mother had just laughed when she told her, but when she told Auntie Kobe about it, she had agreed with Hiro. She was a great believer in the silent communication of minds and such things as reading fortunes from cards.

Well, it wasn't going to hurt anybody to try. Keiko sat on the top step and willed Mike into coming to see her. Fifteen times she told him to come, and then she closed her eyes and said it ten more times. Then, just to give it an extra special touch, she stood up, turned around three times, and said it five more times. When she opened her eyes and looked down the street, there he was—actually, really, and truly coming down the street. It had worked! Hiro was right! Mike was coming and he was pulling a wagon half filled with old newspapers.

Keiko closed her eyes once more, just to have the pleasure of opening them and seeing Mike coming toward her. But when she opened them again, he was gone and only his wagon stood by the curb. She couldn't wait for him to make his way to her. She ran down to the wagon, and in a few minutes Mike came from one of the houses clutching a bundle of old newspapers.

"Mike, I willed you to come see me," Keiko said proudly. "What're you doing?"

Mike didn't seem impressed at all with Keiko's powers. "I'm collecting old newspapers to raise money," he said matter-of-factly. "Does your aunt have some?"

Keiko remembered the rag picker at home who pushed his old cart laden with rags and broken-down pans and umbrellas and dishes

up and down the streets. He asked for old newspapers and magazines too, and Keiko always
tried to help find some because she felt so sorry
for him. And now, here was her friend Mike
doing exactly the same thing.

"I'll help you," she offered. "I'll help you
collect papers."

Mike seemed pleased. "Okay," he said.
"That'll be good," and he pushed the handle of
the wagon into her hand.

"Watch the papers for me while I go to the
next house," he said, and he was gone.

Keiko stood there with the wagon, thinking
how sad it was that Mike should have to collect
old newspapers to help his father earn money.
Maybe if the Chicago wholesaler should cancel
Uncle Henry's orders, she could do the same
thing to help him. What would Mother say if
she heard that Keiko had gone to America and
become a rag picker! Grandmother would be
mortified.

As Keiko stood there grinning at the thought
of what Grandmother would say, a big station wagon pulled up at the curb beside her.
A tall man with short-cropped dark hair,
smoking a pipe, stepped out and smiled at her.

"How's it going?" he asked. "Want me to take what you've got so far?" He moved toward the wagon and started to lift out the papers.

"Those are Mike's!" Keiko said firmly.

The man nodded. "I know," he said. "His mother told me he was out collecting. I'll take what he's got so far."

"No," Keiko said even more firmly. She wasn't going to let any strange man take the papers Mike had collected so far. She moved over and sat down on the pile of papers so that he wouldn't be able to pick them up. He seemed friendly enough, but Mother had always told her not to speak to strangers, and she certainly wasn't going to let this one take what belonged to Mike.

Keiko was glad when she saw Mike coming out with another armload, and she expected the stranger to run off immediately like a thief caught in the act. But he didn't go at all. Instead, he called out to Mike as he came down the walk.

"Hi!" he said. "You've got such a good guard, she won't let me take the papers from your wagon." He laughed good-naturedly, and Mike grinned back at him.

"Hi, Mr. Fletcher," he called. "I just got started."

Mike knew him then! Keiko looked first at Mike and then at the tall stranger and couldn't find a single word to say.

"Mr. Fletcher's our troop leader," Mike explained. "It's okay if he takes the papers."

And then Mr. Fletcher explained how Mike's Scout Troop was collecting newspapers to raise money to fix up their meeting room. The papers weren't to help Mike's father earn money after all. Keiko had made a terrible mistake. She slid off the pile of newspapers feeling very silly.

"My cat is lost," she said meekly, because she couldn't think of anything else to say. "She's black and she came from Japan."

Mr. Fletcher was nice enough to forget about the newspapers and to concentrate on Tama. "I haven't seen any stray cats at all," he said, "but I'll surely keep my eyes open. If she doesn't turn up soon, why not come put an ad in our paper?" Then, wishing them both luck, he put Mike's papers in the back of his station wagon and drove off.

"Bet Mr. Fletcher'd help you find Tama," Mike said quickly. "He's the best writer on the *Richmond Gazette.*"

Until that very minute, it hadn't even occurred to Keiko that she could advertise for Tama.

"I put in an ad for King Arthur when he got lost," Mike went on, "and I got him back in one day. That's the best way to find anything that's lost."

Ideas were beginning to hatch in Keiko's head. "Even people?" she asked.

Mike shrugged. "Never advertised for people," he said.

Suppose Auntie Kobe didn't find Jiro-san in Los Angeles, after all, Keiko thought. And suppose, when she put in an ad for Tama, she just slipped in a few words about Jiro too. Then maybe with one ad Keiko could find both of them. Maybe she would be the one to find Jiro for Auntie Kobe after all. The more she thought about it, the better the idea seemed, and by the time Keiko got home, she had a deep feeling that this was exactly what she should do.

8

An Ad for Tama

Keiko and Mike stood outside the office of the *Richmond Gazette* and peered in through the large plate-glass window. Rain came down in great slanting sheets, and Keiko held an umbrella over their heads with one hand and clutched the two dollars Aunt Emi had given her in the other. She shivered as the cold rain splashed on her cheeks, and she was worried. How was she ever going to explain about Auntie Kobe and Jiro to Mr. Fletcher, when all he thought she'd lost was a black cat? And maybe he wouldn't even remember that. It was all so complicated.

Mike nudged Keiko's arm. "C'mon," he said. "Let's go in."

Then he marched up to the girl who sat at the desk beside the little wooden gate and announced that they had come to see Mr. Fletcher.

The girl scarcely looked up from her typewriter. "Is he expecting you?" she asked.

Of course he wasn't expecting them, Keiko thought. How could he, when he didn't even know they were coming.

"He's my troop leader," Mike said. His voice was not so bold now. "Troop 22," he added meekly.

The girl looked up at Mike, and Keiko saw how her eyebrows made two thin and perfect arches over her wide brown eyes. She looked surprised at everything Mike said to her.

"Say, you kids aren't here to sell Christmas cards or anything, are you?" she asked suspiciously. She looked at Keiko and frowned at the puddle she was making with her wet umbrella.

Mike shook his head. "We came to put in an ad. Mr. Fletcher said we ought to if . . ."

"Oh, why didn't you say so in the first place?" the girl interrupted. "You should see Mrs. Bowen. Alice!" she called.

And now there was another lady standing at the counter to talk with them, and still no one had let them in to see Mr. Fletcher.

Mike didn't look at all happy. "I want to see Mr. Fletcher," he said stubbornly. "He's my troop leader."

And then, as though Mr. Fletcher himself had heard, he came striding toward them from one of the offices in the rear. "Hi!" he called. "Did you find your cat?"

He hadn't forgotten after all. Keiko shook her head. "I came to put in an ad for her and Jiro-san," she said.

Mr. Fletcher looked puzzled. "Oh, did you lose a dog too?" he asked.

Mike thought that was pretty funny. "Jiro-san's a man," he said, and he laughed as though he had just heard a very funny joke. "He's been lost for twenty years."

Mr. Fletcher scratched his head. "Now wait a minute," he said. "Come on in and sit down and start from the beginning."

Then he led them through the gate and to his desk, where he pulled up two chairs. "Now," he said, "tell me just exactly what you are talking about."

There were dozens of desks crowded around Mr. Fletcher's, and everywhere people seemed to be typing or phoning or shuffling through big batches of paper. Mr. Fletcher's own desk was covered with papers too, and his phone seemed to ring every five minutes, but still he listened patiently as Keiko told her story. She started from the beginning, just as he told her to, and she told everything. She told how she

had come to America with Auntie Kobe, how
Auntie Kobe wanted to find her son, how she
had given Tama to her, and how Keiko wanted
to find Tama and Jiro-san more than anything
else. When she finished, she took a deep breath
and added, "I have two dollars for the ad."

Mr. Fletcher rubbed a hand over his chin
and puffed silently on his pipe. "Hmmmm," he
said. "The ad for Tama is simple—but Jiro and
Auntie Kobe. . . . Maybe they would be
material for a feature story. It would be appealing at Christmastime . . ."

Mike leaped to his feet and whistled through
his teeth. "Zowie!" he said. "I told you Mr.
Fletcher'd help."

But Mr. Fletcher calmed him down. "Don't
get too excited, old man," he said to Mike. "I
said maybe. I can't promise. But we'll get the
ad in about Tama for sure, and maybe we'll find
both of them yet."

Keiko felt better already. She couldn't tell
exactly why, but she just had a feeling that
Mr. Fletcher was one of those people with a
good soul, and she knew he would help her if
he could.

When Keiko got home and told what she and
Mike had done, even Uncle Henry was im-

pressed. "Bob Fletcher is a good man," he said. "If he's helping you, you'll probably find both Tama and Jiro-san in no time at all."

Sure enough, the ad for Tama appeared in the *Richmond Gazette* the very next day, but it looked so small and lost, buried among the long list of ads for lost dogs and pet canaries and pearls and handbags, that Keiko was sure no one would ever see it.

"If someone has found Tama, he will be looking for an ad about her," Aunt Emi said, trying to make Keiko feel better. "Don't worry; I'm sure someone will call soon."

And so Keiko waited for someone to call. She waited all day Tuesday and Wednesday and Thursday. She waited until the ad stopped running, and still no one had called.

"Tama is lost forever," Keiko said sadly. "I'll never, never see her again."

But Aunt Emi told her not to give up. "You never can tell about cats," she said. "Maybe some day she will just come home all by herself."

Keiko nodded, but she really didn't think Tama would ever come back now, and deep in her heart she knew she could never quite forgive Uncle Henry for having let her out all alone the very first night she was here. It was really his fault that Tama was lost, Keiko thought glumly, and he had never once said he was sorry.

The only thing that cheered Keiko now was that Christmas was only ten days away. The house was filled with the sound and scent of it, and then one night Uncle Henry brought home a tree that smelled as tangy and fresh as the cool air from the green mountains. Aunt Emi brought up a big cardboard carton from the basement, and after supper they decorated the tree together. Keiko felt as though she were opening a chest full of treasures as she lifted gold and silver and lavender and blue balls from beds of soft white tissue paper.

There were golden stars and glittering snow-flakes; there were tiny silver trumpets and red toadstools. Keiko liked the little wooden angels best, with their polka-dotted wings and their pink hair. They looked like stiff and busy housewives from another world, sprouting wings because they had worked so hard.

"This will be a special Christmas because it is our first one with a daughter," Aunt Emi said happily, and she showed Keiko how to pop

corn and to string it like a ribbon of snow around the tree. She bought boxes of tinsel and tiny canes of real red and white peppermint candy and a new set of lights to brighten the tree.

But even without all this, it would have been a special Christmas for Keiko, because it was the first time she'd ever had a tree all her own. In Tokyo, Grandmother always took them to the Ginza to see the big fat trees in the department stores that wobbled with toys and balls

and long ropes of fuzzy red trimming. But they
had never, never had their own tree at home.
Keiko sat on the floor and looked up now at
the tree that glittered and sparkled just for
her, and she felt the magic of Christmas grow
in her heart. It was the same feeling she had
at home the day before New Year's.

In fact, the house had the same kind of
bright, shivery, exciting feeling of waiting. It
was just that the sounds and smells were different. Instead of the chopping of Mother's knife
on the cutting board and the smell of fish-paste
and bamboo shoots bubbling in soy sauce,
there was the whir of the electric mixer and
the smell of cookies and spice cake baking in
the oven.

Aunt Emi liked to make up boxes of Christmas cookies for the neighbors and Mike's family and the Old People's Home, and, for days
now, the house had smelled like a delicious
bakery. Keiko helped Aunt Emi pack the cookies in boxes with red and green cellophane,
and Aunt Emi let her have any that were
broken or too crisp around the edges. Keiko
got to sample almost all of them that way.

"Hana and Hiro and Kenbo should have gotten my cookies by now, too," Aunt Emi said as

she counted the days since she mailed the big Christmas package to them. "Maybe they're having three o'clock tea and eating some this very minute!"

Keiko tasted the sweet buttery goodness of one of Aunt Emi's crescents and wondered if maybe Hana had just popped one into her mouth too. If only they could all be right here, Keiko thought. She wouldn't even have minded having to look after Kenbo. She would tie him to her back, just as Mother used to do, and take him down to see the lights of Christmas that brightened San Pablo Avenue.

Tiny pricks of loneliness began to flicker through Keiko now, and she wished that Auntie Kobe, at least, were going to be with her for Christmas and New Year's.

But Auntie Kobe had sent a picture post card of a float made entirely of fresh roses, and on it she had written, "I am so discouraged, Kei-chan. The man Captain Sawada told me about was a Jiro, all right, but not mine after all. He had sailed away from Japan on a freighter many years ago, too, and left his mother in Osaka. Can you imagine another Jiro doing the same thing?"

Keiko couldn't imagine. It seemed a shabby

trick that poor Auntie Kobe had gone all the way down to Los Angeles for nothing.

"Since I am here anyway," Auntie Kobe continued, "I am thinking of staying on for New Year's (to see this Tournament of Roses—please see the picture in front), and maybe I shall continue to search here a little longer for Jiro. The priest at the Buddhist temple said he might be able to help me earn some dollars while I am here. (Do you think I could wash dishes? Or perhaps cook American steak?) My love to you all and to Tama, too."

Auntie Kobe's post card was full of long, winding sentences that wound in and out of parentheses, sounding just the way she talked. All it meant in the end, however, was that Auntie Kobe wouldn't be back for the holidays. Keiko was glad now that she had told Mr. Fletcher about Jiro-san. If only he would hurry and write the story, maybe some clues would turn up and then, surely, nothing would keep Auntie Kobe from hurrying back. On the other hand, if there were no story or clues, maybe Auntie Kobe would stay in Los Angeles for weeks or even months. It was not a very happy thought, for now Keiko began to feel that Tama would come back only if Auntie Kobe did.

Once Tama was found, Keiko was sure Jiro-san would turn up too. Somehow they seemed linked together.

The days were growing colder now, and each night Uncle Henry stayed out in the greenhouses till late, checking the temperature, making sure that the steam pipes were in good condition and the boiler was working properly.

Sometimes, when he came in from the cold night, Aunt Emi would make a fresh pot of green tea, and then she would call Keiko and they would sit together in the warm, cozy kitchen, drinking tea, eating the broken cookies from Aunt Emi's tin, and talking about all sorts of things.

These were the times Keiko liked best of all, for sometimes Uncle Henry almost seemed like a different person. The tired lines of worry would ease away from his face, he would lean back and smoke his pipe, and a softness would come into his voice. Then he would ask Keiko about Tokyo and remember about his home in Osaka and tell how different things had been before the war.

When Uncle Henry talked, Aunt Emi listened quietly, but once, when Keiko asked, she spoke of Kyoto and how she and Keiko's mother had grown up there long ago. She talked of the times when the maple trees were gold and they went mushroom hunting in the dark pine forests high in the hills that ringed the city. And she told of springtime when the rice fields were green and the blossoms of the rape plants looked like scattered gold. Sometimes Aunt Emi could paint pictures with her words that sounded almost like the poetry she wrote in the small black notebook she kept in her desk drawer.

But there were other nights, too, when Uncle Henry couldn't stop talking about transplanting and fertilizing and making new cuttings; when he worried about the smog that had made more flowers fold up after they'd reached Chicago, and about the disease that was spreading among the plants in number three greenhouse. He even worried about Keiko's going to school in February.

"You must study at home in the meantime," Uncle Henry said almost sternly one night, "so you will have no trouble when you enter school. After all, you must make a good record your mother will be proud of."

Aunt Emi had borrowed some of Mike's old

school books for Keiko, and she had been working with them a little each day.

"She's really doing very well with Mike's books," Aunt Emi interrupted. "After all, she was best in English in her whole school. I don't think she'll have any difficulty at all."

But Uncle Henry went right on. "You must think ahead about going on to college too, Kei-chan," he said. "You will need good grades for that."

Keiko wrinkled her nose and made a face before she could stop herself. She didn't even want to think about making good grades for going to college. After all, that was years ahead, and, besides, she was only going to stay a year. Uncle Henry didn't know it yet, but by the time next Christmas came, she would be safely back home in Tokyo.

9

The Noise in the Night

It was six nights before Christmas, in the middle of the deepest, darkest part of sleep, when Keiko heard a sound that awakened her. She was dreaming that Mother was actually letting her post the accounts in the ledger and that Hiro was the one who watched. Only half awake, she thought the scratching was the sound of her pen on the paper. But the sound grew louder; and Keiko knew she was in bed in America and that the sound was right outside her window. There was a thud and then a sort of scratching, as though someone were trying to break in. Keiko was sure it must be a thief. Mother always said there were more thieves about at the end of the year when people needed money to pay their debts and buy things for the new year.

Keiko held her breath and listened. There it was again! She was wide awake now and felt shivers race down her back. The thief would probably pry open the window and then crawl into her room. Keiko tried to scream, but her throat was as dry and empty as a cracked clay bowl. She tried to get out of bed and run, but her legs were like two sticks of lead.

"Uncle Henry! Aunt Emi!" she cried, but her voice was so feeble that no one could possibly hear her.

Scratch-scratch . . . scratch-scratch.

The window would surely open soon, and then what would she do? Suddenly, there was an enormous, long "EEeeeeeooooowwwwrrrrr!"

Keiko jumped out of bed and ran to the window, and there, on the window sill, was Tama herself. Her yellow eyes glowed like two small moons, and she arched her back as she rubbed against the window pane. Keiko was so excited that she could scarcely open the window. She fumbled with the lock, reached out, and finally brought Tama safely inside. Her coat was cold and damp, but Keiko hugged Tama close.

"Tama, Tama, where have you been?" she asked softly. "You're safe and you came back in time for Christmas."

She stroked her throat until she heard the rolling *purrrrr,* and then she wrapped her up in her best sweater and started for the door.

Wouldn't Uncle Henry and Aunt Emi be surprised!

She had just turned the knob when she stopped. If she brought Tama in to show them, Uncle Henry would only begin to sneeze again. And besides, he had said he'd be glad if he never saw another cat in the house. What in the world could she do with Tama now that she was safely back?

Keiko carried Tama back into bed with her, pulled the blanket over her head like a tent, and sat cross-legged pondering her problem like an old Indian chief.

"What'll we do, Tama?" she murmured, stroking her silky ears.

If she could just hide her somewhere until Auntie Kobe got back from Los Angeles. Keiko thought of putting her in a carton once more and hiding her in the closet—maybe on the top shelf. But surely Aunt Emi would find her and maybe Uncle Henry would sneeze anyway, even with Tama in the closet. Keiko hunched over, holding Tama tight and thinking very hard. She bit her lip, chewed at a hangnail, and frowned as she tried to have some sort of feeling about what to do.

And then she did something she often tried when she had a particularly difficult problem. She wondered what Hiro would do in her place. In spite of the way he always told her what to do and what not to do, Keiko had to admit that he did possess a great deal of common sense.

Perhaps Hiro would dig a cave for Tama somewhere beyond the greenhouses. He might even build a secret passageway beneath the house for her to hide in. Boys were better at things like that than girls, Keiko thought. And then she remembered Mike. Of course, that was it! She would get Mike to keep Tama for her until Auntie Kobe got back. She would slip out of the house early in the morning and take her to him before anyone was up. Keiko was so pleased with herself for having thought of such a fine idea that she stretched out and promptly fell asleep even before Tama stopped wriggling.

When Keiko woke up the next morning, Aunt Emi was already making breakfast. She was just about to run out with Tama when she heard Uncle Henry's voice.

"Better not work outside today," he was saying to Aunt Emi who had been sniffling with a terrible cold for the last few days.

"You'd better stay in bed and get over that cold before Christmas."

But Aunt Emi just answered, "I'll be all right. Besides, you need help getting the Christmas shipment ready."

Keiko heard Aunt Emi go back to her room, and she waited for Uncle Henry to go outside. She picked Tama up, shoved her under her coat, and stood at the door listening. She could hear the clock measuring out the steady even minutes of the morning. She could hear the water drip-dripping from the faucet. She could smell the crisp brown smell of toast. And then, finally, Uncle Henry did leave. She could hear the back door slam and then his footsteps as he went down the steps.

"Now!" she whispered to Tama, and she slipped from the room, closed the door softly, and ran out the front door like the shadow of a ghost. She held her breath until she was past the house, looking all around in case Uncle Henry should see her. The coast was clear. Keiko took a deep breath and ran the two blocks to Mike's house. She saw him just as he was getting on his bike to go down the street.

"Mike!" she shouted. "Wait!"

Mike turned and beckoned to her to hurry.

"Mom's waiting for milk," he said. "I'm going to the store."

Keiko was so breathless she could hardly speak. She took Tama from beneath her bulging coat and thrust her into Mike's arms. "H-h-h-here," she said, still panting. "Keep her for me."

Mike looked as though he'd been hit on the head with a baseball bat. "Hey," he said. "You found your cat. You found Tama!"

Keiko could only nod. And finally she had breath enough to tell him how Tama had come home in the middle of the night and scratched at her window.

Mike rubbed the top of his head. "Well, whaddaya know!" he said, and he looked at Tama as though he still couldn't believe it.

"Uncle Henry won't want her around because she'll make him sneeze," Keiko went on, "so keep her for me till Auntie Kobe comes back?"

Mike knew about Uncle Henry's not liking cats. He remembered what he had said that day he'd brought back three from the Humane Society. Still, he did have his own dog and a tank full of tropical fish.

"Maybe she'll fight with King Arthur," Mike said doubtfully, "or eat my fish."

Keiko didn't have time to argue with him. "They won't fight," she said firmly, just as Auntie Kobe might have done. "And I just know she won't eat the fish. She's a very responsible cat." She sounded more than ever like Auntie Kobe.

Mike looked down at Tama and shrugged. "Maybe I can teach her to do tricks," he said. "Maybe I can start an animal act with her and King Arthur."

Mike was full of impossible ideas, but Keiko didn't have time to listen. "Take good care of her for me," she said. "She likes dried fish. And don't tell anybody you have her. It's a secret." Then she turned and ran home as fast as she could go.

Keiko could hardly wait to tell Aunt Emi. She would be so pleased and surprised. She ran up the steps, burst into the kitchen, and found it looking exactly as it had when she left.

"Aunt Emi?" she called.

Aunt Emi was in bed with a thermometer in her mouth. "Stay away, Kei-chan," she called.

"I think I have the flu. The doctor is coming."

And when the doctor did come later, with his black bag bulging with tongue depressors and bottles of pink and white capsules, he told Uncle Henry that Aunt Emi was very sick. In fact, he said she had pneumonia and should go to a hospital immediately.

Uncle Henry looked pale and worried, almost as though he were sick himself. He wandered from room to room not knowing what to do, and Keiko sat scrunched up on the couch watching him and wishing she had that medicine in those little blue bottles right now. It would be a medicine people could take so that they wouldn't have to go to hospitals, Keiko thought.

It was Mike's mother, Mrs. Michaelson, who came hurrying in from the packing house to cheer them both up. She wore wool slacks and a sweater, and short sandy-colored curls tumbled all over her head.

"Your aunt will get well much faster in the hospital, Keiko," she said brightly. "And until she comes back, how would you like to come stay with us? We'll put Mike in with his brother Ben, and you can have Mike's room. How would that be?"

Keiko couldn't think of anything nicer, and Uncle Henry seemed grateful too. And so that afternoon, Keiko packed her suitcase once more and Mike carried it home for her on the handle bars of his bike.

"We'll take good care of her," Mike's mother said to Uncle Henry.

Mike's house wasn't at all like Aunt Emi and Uncle Henry's. It was bulging with collections and pets of all kinds. Mike's mother had a wrought-iron stand full of African violets that bloomed in single and double petals of pink and white and lavender. Those were near the living-room window. And then in the dining room, she had a cupboard full of white milk glass that spilled over onto the table, where a milk glass bowl was filled with barley sugar candy. Mr. Michaelson had bowling trophies on top of the mantel and the bookshelf, and fishing rods standing in the hall. The case of mounted butterflies and the rock collection from Bolinas Beach belonged to Mike's brother Ben. All the live pets belonged to Mike. There was the tank of tropical fish in his bedroom right beneath the photograph of Mike and Ben at Scout Camp; there was the dishpan with Mike's pet turtle, Herbert, and there was a cage in the kitchen with the para-keets, Susie and Buster. In the midst of all the clutter, Tama was curled up happily on the couch, looking as though she had always lived there.

"We all love Tama," Mrs. Michaelson said enthusiastically. "Mike told me we were to keep her until your friend, Auntie Kobe, came back from Los Angeles."

Of course Mike had had to tell about Tama. He hadn't been able to keep it a secret after all.

"Did he tell about Uncle Henry's not liking her, too?" she asked.

Mrs. Michaelson nodded. "It's a shame Henry is allergic to cats," she said with a frown. "How sad that would be!"

And before Keiko quite knew what she was doing, she found herself sitting on the couch next to Mike's mother, telling her all her troubles. "Uncle Henry doesn't like me either," she blurted out. "All he likes are his carna-tions!"

Mike's mother moved closer and put an arm around Keiko. "That's not so at all, Keiko," she said gently. "Your uncle just doesn't know how to show you, but he loves you very much. I know. You'll find out someday too."

Keiko wondered if she were right. If Uncle Henry really loved her, he certainly hadn't shown it at all. At least, not yet.

It was strange going to sleep in Mike's room that night. It was peculiar to see the shadows of his ship's model looming darkly on the wall and to see all those model airplanes hanging from the ceiling, as though a formation of planes had suddenly descended over her head. But the one nice thing—the very nicest possible thing—was that Tama was sleeping in the room with her.

"You can let her sleep in there," Mike had said generously, "but she can't have King Arthur's bed." And he went to the basement and brought up a carton that had once held a dozen bottles of catsup.

Keiko let Tama creep into bed with her for a little while, just because she was so glad to have her back again. She meant to put her back in the box in a minute, but she fell asleep still holding Tama in her arms. And it was Tama's sneezing and wheezing that woke Keiko up in the middle of the night.

Keiko had opened the window before she'd gone to bed, and now she could feel the cold dampness of the night air. No wonder Tama had caught cold. Keiko leaped out of bed to close the window and sniffed the strange smell in the air outside. The night was still and windless and Keiko felt as though she could almost see the chemicals and gases that would burn Uncle Henry's carnations again. She knew his big Christmas shipment was to go out the next afternoon, too. Suppose it was smog and suppose the flowers were ruined tonight, then maybe there would be nothing worth shipping to Chicago tomorrow. Uncle Henry might not only lose his Christmas order but also the orders for the rest of the year. Keiko sat on her bed and wondered what to do. Tama sat beside her sneezing and wheezing as though telling her to hurry. Keiko looked at the clock. It was one o'clock, and Mike's house was as still as a tomb. Suppose she woke everybody up and they just thought she was being silly.

Keiko thought for another minute, and then knew she had to tell Uncle Henry. She got up quickly, put on her bathrobe, and knocked on Mike's door. It would be easiest to tell him first.

"Mike!" she called softly. "Wake up."

But the house was still as silent as a tomb.

This time Keiko shouted and banged on the door. "Mike, wake up!"

Ben popped his head out of the door. "What's wrong?" he asked.

"What is it? What's the matter, Keiko?" This time it was Mike's father and then his mother calling from the next room.

Soon, even King Arthur came sleepily out the door, squeaking as he yawned an enormous yawn and stretching as he wagged his tail. He thought it was morning and time to have breakfast.

Keiko had managed to awaken everybody except Mike. She quickly told Mr. and Mrs. Michaelson about the funny smell outside and about Tama's sneezing and about how Aunt Emi had said maybe they could have saved most of the shipment the last time if they'd only cut the flowers in time.

Mike's father shrugged with a sleepy look. "I'm inclined to let things go till morning, myself," he said. "I don't think a few hours could make much difference."

But Mike's mother went to the window, opened it, and sniffed. "It does smell odd," she said thoughtfully. She remembered what had happened the last time too, and she saw Tama wheezing and brushing at her nose with one white paw.

"I know Henry would hate to lose even part of this shipment," she said. "Maybe I'd better call him."

By now, Mike was up too. "What's wrong?" he asked. "I'm hungry." And he promptly fixed himself a bowl of corn flakes with strawberry jam and milk, while his mother went to the telephone to call Uncle Henry.

Keiko wouldn't have minded a bowl of corn flakes herself—especially with strawberry jam —but she wanted to hear what Mike's mother said. Mrs. Michaelson told Uncle Henry how Tama had wakened them with her sneezing and about the funny smell outside.

"I thought, with the Christmas shipment at stake, you might want to get them cut," she added. She was silent a moment, listening and nodding, and then when she hung up, she called out, "Get dressed everybody. Henry's decided not to take a chance. We're all going over to help him cut his flowers."

"Tonight?" Ben asked. "Right now?"

"Me too?" Mike asked, surprised. No one ever asked him to help at the nursery. Usually, he was told to stay out of the way.

"Yes, you too, Mike," his mother answered. "We're all going right now. Henry can't call his other workers at midnight, and we're all up anyway, so I told him we'd come. Put on your warm slacks and coat, Keiko," she said.

And in fifteen minutes they had all bundled out of the house, climbed into the big station wagon, and roared over to Uncle Henry's. The greenhouses were bleak and dark, and the paths between them were like black ribbons of night. Keiko followed close after Mike, watching the wobbly beam of light made by his flashlight. Their footsteps scrunched on the pebbly path and, at last, Keiko saw a faint light in one of the greenhouses, where Uncle Henry was already at work cutting the flowers. They found him working quickly, cutting deftly with a sharp thrust of his pocket knife, leaving enough young shoots on each stalk for later blooms. On the ground beside him was a piece of newspaper already piled high with the flowers he had cut.

"Tama woke me up," Keiko called out to him. "She came through the window and tonight the smog made her sneeze and she woke me up and I smelled a funny smell, so I called Mike and his mother phoned you and we all came." Keiko couldn't seem to stop once she'd got started.

Uncle Henry nodded. "Well," he said, "so Tama is home and she smelled the smog. Well!" And then he was back at work again as though he couldn't waste another minute. "We'd better hurry," he said.

Mike's mother told everyone what to do. "Ben, you and Dad and I will help Henry cut the flowers," she said. "Mike can carry them to the packing house, and if there's time, I'll start grading them."

"With four of us cutting, we should be able to cover most of the greenhouses in a couple of hours," Mike's father said. Quickly Uncle Henry began to show him how to cut properly.

"We need more newspaper cushions too, Kei-chan," Uncle Henry said, as though she would know exactly what to do.

Keiko didn't know what in the world Uncle Henry was talking about, but Mike said he'd show her. "C'mon," he said, and he darted out toward the packing house, his flashlight bobbing up and down like a summer glowworm.

Keiko felt the dampness all around and shivered. "Wait," she called. "Wait for me," and she ran after him as fast as she could go. She wasn't going to be left behind in the spooky shadows of the greenhouses.

Mike took her to a table piled high with newspapers and showed her how to roll a few sheets together and tuck in the ends to make neat, soft rolls. They would be put inside the big cartons to cushion the flowers as they were packed. "See," he said. "It's simple."

Keiko nodded. It was simple. Hana, or maybe even Kenbo, could have done it. Keiko wanted to show Uncle Henry how fast she could work. She sat at the table and rolled and rolled newspapers until her arms ached, her hands were smudgy with printer's ink, and she could scarcely keep her eyes open.

Mike helped her for a while, and then he ran back and forth between the packing house and the greenhouses with the flowers that had been cut. He even stripped some of the low leaves from the stems, just as he had seen his mother and Keiko's aunt do.

After a while, Mrs. Michaelson hurried back to begin work at the grading table. "Come help me, Keiko," she called.

Keiko was so surprised that she nearly fell as she hurried from the stool. Mrs. Michaelson

was asking her to do the work Aunt Emi herself would have done if she were here.

"The long-stemmed number ones go here,"
she explained, "the shorter ones there, and
the very shortest here. We put twenty-five in a
bunch, and then Mike can put them in buckets
for us." Even while she talked, her hands flew
as she sorted the flowers.

Of course, Keiko couldn't begin to keep up

with her. She picked up the flowers carefully
—more carefully than she had ever handled
flowers in Mother's shop. There must have
been hundreds of them on the grading table
now. There were Uncle Henry's prize-winning
White Sims, his beautiful Red Sims, and there
were others that were pink and lemon-colored
and even white with red stripes. They smelled
like spring and sunshine, and they made

Keiko's heart sing, they were so beautiful. And suddenly, Keiko knew why Uncle Henry took such good care of his plants. She knew then why he loved them as much as she loved Tama. And she remembered what her father had once said about his own dwarf pine.

"You must love the tree enough almost to become the tree yourself. Then you will know how to care for it, and it will flourish and grow and be beautiful for you."

Keiko hadn't understood at all then, but now she thought she understood a little. Maybe she was beginning to understand Uncle Henry a little too.

When Uncle Henry and Mr. Michaelson had finished cutting all the flowers at last, they came back to the packing house. Keiko could see out of the corner of her eye that Uncle Henry looked pleased to see her standing next to Mike's mother, working just as Aunt Emi would have done. She was working much harder than Mike or Ben who were clowning together in the corner of the packing house, having a duel with two wads of rolled newspapers. And she felt proud and important to be working so hard at four in the morning. It was as though she were a doctor performing a midnight operation that would save someone's life.

When all the flowers had been graded and bunched and put into buckets, Uncle Henry and Mike's father carried them into the big storage icebox. They would be safe there until they could be packed in the large Fiberglas lined cartons that would keep them from freezing as they flew to Chicago.

"We'll get these flowers packed with your newspaper cushions first thing tomorrow morning," Uncle Henry said to Keiko, and, though he looked tired, he seemed happier than he had in a long time.

They all went inside then, and Mike's mother made hot coffee and cocoa for everybody, and somehow, even the tiredness felt good.

"I don't know how to thank you," Uncle Henry said, shaking hands with Mr. and Mrs. Michaelson. "This is a bad case of smog. You've helped me save most of my Christmas shipment, and maybe the rest of the orders for the year as well."

"It was Keiko who woke us up," Mrs. Michaelson said quickly.

"And it was Tama who woke *me* up," Keiko added. She wanted to be sure Tama would get proper credit.

"I'm very grateful," Uncle Henry said solemnly, "to all of you. To Tama too." And he shook hands with Mike and Ben and even Keiko.

Then they all said good night and climbed into the station wagon, and Uncle Henry stood at the curb watching as they drove away. Keiko looked back as they turned the corner and saw that he still stood there, all alone, waving in the half light. He looked tired and lonely, and Keiko knew she hadn't been a very good daughter to leave him all alone.

10

Being a Good Daughter

Now that Tama was safe at home once more, Keiko had a funny feeling that Jiro-san would turn up before long too. Each day since she and Mike had gone to see Mr. Fletcher, she had been watching the *Richmond Gazette*, but so far there had been nothing.

"Maybe he forgot," Keiko said to Mike as they looked through the paper together.

"Or maybe he's saving it for the Christmas edition," Mike said hopefully. "He said it'd be appealing at Christmastime."

Secretly, Keiko thought that was exactly what he would do, but she didn't dare say it out loud, because then maybe it wouldn't happen.

Mike's mother told both of them to be patient. "After all, Mr. Fletcher is a busy man," she said, "and I imagine he has a great deal on his mind besides your story."

Keiko knew she was right, but she hoped there might be a little something in his mind that would remind him of the story about Jiro-san.

Aunt Emi was feeling better now, but the doctor told her to stay in the hospital a few more days just to make sure. Keiko wrote to tell her how much she missed her and about Tama's coming home. Then, just to show her that Tama was really and truly right there beside her, Mike helped her ink the bottom of Tama's paw and together they pressed it on one of the letters. Under the inky blue paw print Keiko wrote, "Love from Tama, too. Meowr!"

The only trouble with that was that Tama got away before they could blot her paws and left little inky paw prints all over the floor of Mike's room. It was a good thing the floor was covered with linoleum so that they could wipe it up before Mrs. Michaelson saw what happened. After they had cleaned up the mess, Keiko drew Christmas angels and bells and snowflakes all around the edges of Aunt Emi's letter. And if Aunt Emi weren't home by Christmas, she thought, she would send her the tortoise-shell comb that came wrapped in red silk in a small wooden box. Mother had told her to use it for a present someday.

On Christmas Eve Mrs. Michaelson called

up Uncle Henry and told him to come have dinner with them.

"I won't hear of you sitting there by yourself eating cold rice," she said. But Uncle Henry said something had gone wrong with the rotor tiller, and he wanted to fix it before the man came to work with it after Christmas.

Mike's mother shook her head. "I never saw a man who worked so hard," she said. "Keiko, will you take some fried chicken to him? And see if he won't come over after he's been to the hospital to see Aunt Emi."

Keiko would go, of course, but she did wish someone could go with her. Nights came early now, and already it was growing dark. Mike was still out on his paper route, however, and Ben was busy in the basement trying to repair a string of lights that had gone out on the tree. Mike had taken King Arthur with him, and Keiko knew Uncle Henry wouldn't appreciate her bringing Tama along. She looked around. Surely there was something she could take along for company.

And then she saw little Herbert sitting on the smooth round stone in the middle of his dishpan. Mike wouldn't mind if she carried him over and brought him right back. Keiko scooped him up and put him in her pocket, and then she hurried to Uncle Henry's house.

The wind was cold, and already three stars had popped out in the sky. It was comforting to feel Herbert in her pocket and to talk to him as she hurried along. The fried chicken beneath the clean white napkin smelled good, and Keiko wanted to hurry back to have her own dinner at Mike's.

She went around to the back yard first, expecting to see Uncle Henry puttering in the shed or stringing up some of the carnations in the greenhouses. She looked all around but didn't see him anywhere. Then the light went on in the kitchen. She hurried in and discovered he'd been there all along but had just been too busy to turn on the lights. He had cooked some rice, and it had sputtered and boiled over and now was burned and black.

"I brought you some fried chicken," Keiko said, holding out the basket. "It's from Mike's mother."

Uncle Henry seemed pleased. "Well," he said. "That was very nice of her . . . and of you to bring it," he added. He didn't seem to know what else to say.

"Mike's mother says for you to come over

after you've been to see Aunt Emi," Keiko went on. If only they would let children visit the hospital, she could have gone with him.

It seemed strange for the two of them to be talking in the kitchen without Aunt Emi. Somehow, it wasn't comfortable at all. It was like standing on tiptoe too long, straining and reaching for something you couldn't quite see.

Uncle Henry seemed to be waiting for Keiko to say something more, so she dug into her pocket and produced Herbert.

"This is Mike's turtle," she said, holding him out. "I borrowed him for just a little while."

Uncle Henry took Herbert, studied his yellow painted back, and then smiled. "How is Tama?" he asked, as though something on Herbert's yellow back had made him think of her.

"She's fine," Keiko answered cautiously. She wasn't quite sure what Uncle Henry was leading up to.

It turned out, however, that he wasn't leading up to anything at all. "How would you like to stay and keep me company for supper?" he asked suddenly. He looked at the chicken Mike's mother had sent and said, "Looks like there's enough for both of us."

Keiko thought of Mike's house with the Christmas tree all lighted up and a fire in the fireplace and the smell of chicken frying in the kitchen. She thought of Tama lapping up a saucer of milk under the stove and of King Arthur wagging his tail as he chewed on a bone. More than anything, Keiko wanted to run back and be a part of that warm, cozy Christmasy house.

"We can light up the tree," Uncle Henry went on. "With you gone, I'd even forgotten to turn on the lights. I could drop you off at Mike's on the way to the hospital."

Keiko knew Uncle Henry wanted her to stay. Already he was going to the cupboard to get a plate for her. How could she say no and leave him all alone?

"All right," Keiko said. "I'll stay."

Uncle Henry went to phone Mike's mother, and Keiko could tell by the things he said that Mrs. Michaelson didn't think there was enough chicken. "There's plenty here," Uncle Henry kept saying. "There's plenty for two. Thank you. Thank you very much." And on the way back to the kitchen, he plugged in the tree lights. Now Keiko's own tree was bright and shining too.

They sat down at the kitchen table, and Uncle Henry served his burned-smelling rice with brown streaks trailing through it. He had just put a piece of chicken on Keiko's plate when the door bell rang.

"You begin eating," he said as he went to the door. "I'll be back in a minute."

Keiko looked at her cold chicken and burned rice and sighed. It was hard trying to be a good daughter to Uncle Henry. And then she heard a laugh. She would have known it anywhere. She ran out to the living room, and it was—it really was—Auntie Kobe herself!

She hugged Keiko close and laughed in her ear. "I just couldn't spend Christmas and New Year's away from my little Kei-chan," she said. "I came back on a bus, and do you know I didn't even go to Mrs. Fuji's? I came straight here."

"Oh, Auntie Kobe," Keiko said over and over again. "You came back. You're really here! And Tama's back too, and if Mr. Fletcher writes the story, maybe Jiro-san will come back too."

Poor Auntie Kobe didn't know what in the world Keiko was talking about.

"Wait, wait. . . . What are you talking

about? Where has Tama been?" she asked. "And who is Mr. Fletcher and where is your auntie? My, I smell rice burning!" She took off her coat and hat and bustled into the kitchen, sniffing and saying that something most certainly was burning.

"It's the rice," Uncle Henry said faintly, but no one paid much attention, for Keiko was trying to tell how Aunt Emi was in the hospital, and how Tama was lost, and how she'd come back in the middle of the night. She even told about Mr. Fletcher's promising to write a story to help find Jiro.

When Keiko stopped for breath, Uncle Henry told how Tama and Keiko had gotten everyone up and helped save most of the Christmas crop from smog damage. "They all came over in the middle of the night to help me," Uncle Henry went on, and Keiko noticed how proud he seemed.

She had never heard Uncle Henry talk like that before. In fact, he hadn't said anything very special to her at all since that night. And now, here he was talking to Auntie Kobe just the way Mother talked when any of the children had done something especially fine.

What's more, he had the same pleased look on his face.

And all the while, Auntie Kobe sat there nodding and beaming. "Keiko is a most responsible child," she said with great authority, "and Tama is an exceptional cat."

Naturally, with the food just sitting there in front of her, Auntie Kobe had to be invited to dinner. She lifted the lid of the rice pan and sniffed as she peered inside. She took one look at the three pieces of chicken on the plate and shook her head sadly. *"Mah,"* she said, "if I had only known, I would have come back days ago."

And so Keiko had to explain that she was staying at Mike's and that the plate of chicken had just been meant for Uncle Henry.

"Never mind," Uncle Henry said. "I can still make this a good feast," and he went to the cupboard and brought back a can of peas, a can of applesauce, and a can of Japanese pickles. He spread everything out on the table and then urged, "Now, please eat."

Keiko didn't even care about the food now. It was so good to have Auntie Kobe sitting right there beside her, telling about Los Angeles and how she had seen Captain Sawada and the officers of the *Nikko Maru*. It was as though Keiko were being rewarded for having been a good daughter to Uncle Henry.

Auntie Kobe told about the Jiro who turned out to be another Jiro altogether, and about the Buddhist temple and the kind priest there. "It was a nice trip," she said thoughtfully, "even though I didn't find my Jiro."

When Auntie Kobe had eaten the last pea on her plate, Keiko blurted out, "Auntie Kobe, Tama makes Uncle Henry sneeze."

Auntie Kobe didn't seem surprised at all. "Ah," she said knowingly, "so that is it. I knew from the very first moment I saw you that there was some reason why you didn't like cats. Of course you wouldn't if they make you sneeze."

Uncle Henry shook his head. "It is something I have been trying to cure with shots at the allergy clinic," he explained. "I have been going for treatments since the day after Tama arrived."

All Keiko could do was sit there and stare at Uncle Henry. Why, he had never once said anything about that either. And if he were going for treatments, that meant he didn't mind if she had a cat.

"Then can I keep Tama here?" she asked. "You won't care if she lives here too?" It seemed too good to be true.

Uncle Henry didn't answer her. He just got up from the table and went to his room. When he came back, he handed Keiko a small paper bag.

"This was going to be my Christmas present for Tama," he said, "but I might as well give it to you right now."

Inside the bag was a small red leather collar with a silver bell and a brass tag on which Tama's name had been printed in big block letters. And below her name was the address in case she should ever get lost again. This was Uncle Henry's way of telling Keiko she could keep Tama for always.

"After all," he said, smiling, "where else could I find a cat who warns me of smog? She's a pretty valuable cat, I'd say."

Keiko was so happy that she couldn't think of a single thing to say. "Oh, Uncle Henry," she said over and over again, "thank you ten million times!"

Mike's mother was right after all. He did care, about her and about Tama too. And Keiko knew

she was never going to think mean thoughts about Uncle Henry again, ever.

"So Tama will live here happily ever after," Auntie Kobe said as though she were telling the end of a wonderful story. "And now, what is all this about Mr. Fletcher?"

When Keiko told how she had tried to put something about Jiro-san in the newspapers for her, Auntie Kobe seemed close to tears. "*Mah*, you are a sweet child," she said.

That was what made Keiko say the story would be in the Christmas edition. "That's what Mr. Fletcher said," Keiko added, even though she knew very well he had told Mike he couldn't promise a thing.

"And tomorrow is Christmas," Auntie Kobe said. "If it is in tomorrow's paper, perhaps Jiro will see it somewhere and perhaps by New Year's he will be right here. Oh, Kei-chan!" she said, clasping her hands together.

Keiko was sorry she'd opened her mouth. Now, suppose it wasn't in the paper tomorrow after all. Suppose Mr. Fletcher had forgotten all about it and it would never be in the paper!

But as Keiko sat there thinking gloomy thoughts, Uncle Henry said it was time for him to be going to the hospital. Auntie Kobe phoned Mrs. Fuji to tell her she was back, but that she must stay here until Aunt Emi came home. "After all," she said, "I can't leave little Kei-chan and her uncle to eat burned rice and canned peas every day."

Since Auntie Kobe was going to stay, Keiko would move back from Mike's, and it was decided Uncle Henry would take them both to the Michaelsons' so that Keiko could pick up Tama and her suitcase.

The Michaelsons were almost as excited as Keiko when they met Auntie Kobe, for Keiko had told Mike all about her, and Mike had told Ben and his mother and father.

"It's as though we've known you all along," Mike's mother said as she shook Auntie Kobe's hand.

And then Mike said, "Herbert's gone. Do you know where he is?"

Keiko had forgotten all about him. She felt in her pocket, but there was only a little damp spot where she had carried him. She felt in one pocket and then the other. She had taken him out to show Uncle Henry and then what had happened? Where had Uncle Henry put him? After all Mike had done to help find Tama, she'd taken his turtle without even asking and had lost him on top of that.

"I . . . I borrowed him," Keiko admitted.

"Well, where is he?" Mike asked. "I saved him a good piece of hamburger from lunch."

"I think . . . I think he's in the sink at Uncle Henry's," Keiko said at last. That sounded like a nice wet spot a turtle would like, and that seemed to satisfy Mike too.

"Okay then," he said. "You can keep him till tomorrow, but be careful with him. And here," he said, handing Keiko a greasy little wad of paper in which he'd kept his piece of hamburger. "Feed him this for his supper."

Keiko nodded. She could hardly wait to get back home now to look for Herbert.

"It will be nice for your uncle to have the two of you staying with him," Mike's mother said, "even though it's been fun having Keiko here."

She insisted that they have some apple pie and ice cream for dessert, and then Mr. Michaelson took Keiko and Auntie Kobe and Tama home in the station wagon.

The first thing Keiko did was to run to the sink to look for Herbert, but all she found there was a stack of dirty dishes.

"Maybe he is crawling about somewhere," Auntie Kobe suggested, and the two of them got down on their hands and knees and looked all over the kitchen floor. Keiko got Uncle Henry's flashlight, and they even looked under the beds and the couch and under every piece of furniture in the house. But Herbert just wasn't to be found.

"Well, he will turn up," Auntie Kobe said, consoling Keiko. "He will turn up just the way Tama did."

But Keiko couldn't wait weeks for Herbert. Mike would ask for him tomorrow!

Something to Celebrate

Keiko knew that Christmas would turn out to be a terrible day if she didn't find Herbert. But she did. She found him right after breakfast, and she found him because Uncle Henry and Auntie Kobe and she all put their minds to it.

"Now think," Auntie Kobe had said. "Think about every little thing you said and did last night when you had Herbert."

And so Keiko and Uncle Henry thought about how they stood in the kitchen and how Uncle Henry had taken Herbert and looked at his yellow back and asked about Tama.

"And what were you wearing?" Auntie Kobe asked.

That was when Uncle Henry thought of his green sweater. "That's right, by George," he said. "I had on that sweater." And he hurried to his room to get his sweater. He felt in his pocket, and that was where Herbert had spent the night, hanging in Uncle Henry's closet.

Keiko knew then that it would be a good

day. Grandmother always said that if something good happened first thing in the morning, it would be a good day. Maybe Mr. Fletcher's story would really be in the paper today, Keiko thought, and maybe the doctor would suddenly decide to send Aunt Emi home.

It did turn out to be a fine day, all right, but not in exactly the way Keiko had expected. The first thing she did was to feed Herbert his hamburger dinner for breakfast and put him in a dishpan of water with a stone to rest on. Then there were all the wonderful presents— a blue sweater and skirt from Uncle Henry and Aunt Emi, red beads from Auntie Kobe, and a book about American Indians from Mike.

At three o'clock they were all invited to the Michaelsons' for Christmas dinner. There was roast turkey with cranberry sauce, candied yams, peas and carrots, a salad of peach halves filled with cream cheese, and a pumpkin pie Mike's mother had baked herself. It was the biggest and most fabulous dinner Auntie Kobe or Keiko had ever, ever eaten. It was the kind of dinner one might expect at the Imperial Hotel in Tokyo. Of course Keiko had never eaten there. In fact, she hadn't ever been inside, but she guessed that even a dinner there couldn't have been better than the one Mike's mother had made. It left you feeling good inside and out, and Mrs. Michaelson put aside a few slices of turkey and a piece of pie to be taken to Aunt Emi later. They all signed a card to go with it, telling her they missed her, and to get well soon.

Mike had to go off on his paper route then, and shortly after he left, they heard the thud of the paper on the porch. Mr. Michaelson brought it in and let Keiko open it because he knew she had been waiting all afternoon for it.

"It just might be in there today," he said, and he handed it to her with an encouraging smile. Then he and Uncle Henry watched a program on television while she looked at the paper from cover to cover.

Auntie Kobe stood peering over her shoulder. "Have you found it yet?" she asked. "Is it there?"

But there wasn't anything at all in it about Jiro-san who had been lost for twenty long years. The Christmas edition, instead of being thick and fat and filled with interesting stories as Keiko thought it might be, was even thinner and flatter than usual. Keiko saw the disappointment on Auntie Kobe's face and felt miserable.

"Never mind, Kei-chan," Auntie Kobe said quietly. "There are other ways we can look for him."

This made Keiko feel even worse, for it sounded as though she didn't expect Mr. Fletcher to write about him, ever.

Altogether, it wasn't such a happy day after all, Keiko thought—that is, until Mike came home. Mike's grandmother in Michigan had sent him a brand-new football for Christmas. Mike had told her how he and Ben and even his father had played with it all morning. Now, Mike twirled it between his palms and tried to get Ben to go out and play with it again.

"C'mon, Benjie," he said, "just for a little while. C'mon, Benjamin, just catch a couple with me," he coaxed.

But Ben was watching television too, and he didn't want to go. "Go away," he said to Mike. "Not now." And Ben wouldn't move.

Keiko watched Mike twirl the ball around and around. She knew he was aching to go outside with it, but he couldn't very well play catch alone. "Want me to go?" she asked in a small voice.

Mike looked at her, and then he looked at Ben, and then at his football, and finally, reluctantly, he said, "Okay. Let's go then."

Keiko didn't mind if she was last choice. She knew Freddy and Skipper down the street had gone to their grandmother's in San Francisco. She knew Mike had thought of everybody he could possibly ask before he agreed to take her. Still she didn't mind at all.

Mike looked up and down the street to make sure none of the boys were around. Then he told Keiko to back off. "Way back," he called. He lifted his arm and with a quick thrust whirled the ball toward Keiko. It took ten tries before she learned how to hang onto the slippery curve of the ball, and it bounced crazily every which way down the street whenever she missed. The football was just as hard to throw as it was to catch, but Mike was so glad to have somebody to play catch with that he didn't get mad once.

That night Keiko wrote a letter and addressed it especially to Hiro. She told all about Christmas, of course; about Auntie Kobe's coming back, about the red collar for Tama from Uncle Henry, about the big dinner at Mike's and all the wonderful presents. Then at the very end she wrote, "And I played football today with my friend Mike."

When Keiko read the letter over, she knew that wasn't exactly true. But it did sound impressive. She grinned just thinking how Hiro's eyes would pop when he read that. "P.S.," she wrote. "It was a brand-new football from Mike's grandmother in Michigan." And she drew a picture of herself throwing it for Kenbo to see.

Aunt Emi came home the day before New Year's. She looked rested and her eyes were bright, and she said she felt better than she had in a long, long time. But Auntie Kobe insisted on staying to do the cooking and cleaning for another week at least, and that was how she happened to make a real Japanese feast for them on New Year's Day. It was almost as good as the New Year's feast Mother made, only, of course, most of the things had to come out of cans or from the Japanese grocer's truck. Keiko couldn't run to the store to buy squid or lotus root or herring roe. Instead, Auntie Kobe bought sea bass and burdock root and bean-curd cakes and fish-paste from Mr. Ito, who came around in his rattly old truck bulging with vegetables and wooden crates and dangling scales and paper bags. He even had rice cakes for the special New Year's broth.

This time the Michaelsons all came to their house. Mike even brought King Arthur because he wouldn't stay home and Herbert just because he happened to be in his pocket.

Uncle Henry didn't sneeze once, and although he said the shots he'd been taking each week were beginning to work, Auntie Kobe said it was because she had been mixing some packets of white powders from her medicine box in his coffee the past few mornings.

Uncle Henry slapped his thigh and shook his head. "No wonder," he said. "I thought the coffee tasted terrible, but I didn't dare say anything."

Auntie Kobe thought she had played a pretty good trick on Uncle Henry, and she laughed until she grew weak and had to sit down.

"You did right," Aunt Emi said, nodding. "He never would have taken the medicine any other way. And he *has* stopped sneezing." And he surely had.

In fact, ever since Christmas Uncle Henry had scarcely looked cross or worried at all. The farm adviser from the university had brought him a new spray that stopped the disease in the cuttings, and the wholesaler in Chicago had doubled his orders for the rest of the year. Uncle Henry had already ordered the new washer for Aunt Emi as a sort of welcome home present from the hospital, and he had gone out to buy Keiko a new gray coat with a velvet collar. He had bought her a new pair of saddle shoes for school too. Keiko wrapped them in tissue and put them back in the box just as they had come. She wanted to keep the shoes new and clean so they would last forever, like the clogs her teacher had given her at home.

Everyone told Auntie Kobe she was the best cook of Japanese New Year's food ever to come along. Mr. and Mrs. Michaelson ate some of everything on the big platters, but Mike didn't like the herring roe and Ben didn't like the fish-paste. Keiko took a little of everything, as she usually did at home, and it was just like New Year's in Tokyo.

After dinner, there were the Bowl games to see on television, and by now Mike's foot-

ball was old enough so that he would rather watch the games than go out and play ball with Keiko.

But Keiko didn't mind because Tama did the most wonderful thing that could have happened. She went out to the greenhouses all alone, and when she came back in, she brought a mouse. And then she did something even more wonderful. Instead of dropping it in front of Keiko as anyone would have expected, she took it straight to Uncle Henry and dropped it on the toe of his right shoe, as though she knew he was the one person who would appreciate it most. And, of course, he was.

"Say," he burst out, "this is probably the

rascal who has been nipping off the buds in number two greenhouse. He was too clever for cheese in a trap, but I guess Tama was too smart for him."

And he talked to Tama and told her what a good cat she was and rubbed under her chin. And Tama knew he was pleased. She calmly picked up the mouse again and went outside, as though everything was all right now.

"Pretty useful cat you have there," Mike's father said, grinning.

"Boy, she's the smartest cat I ever saw," Mike said.

"Lots better than a mousetrap," Ben added.

And Keiko thought she would burst with pride as Uncle Henry nodded and said, "We're lucky to have her all right. She's a good little cat."

Aunt Emi and Mike's mother agreed, as soon as they were sure the mouse was safely out of the house, but Auntie Kobe seemed the most pleased of all. "I knew she belonged right here with Keiko," she said contentedly. "I just felt it in my bones all along."

It was just after the Michaelsons had gone home that the telephone rang. Uncle Henry had thrown another log on the fire, and the shower of sparks against the black soot of the chimney had set Keiko to thinking about the fireworks on the Sumida River. The Christmas tree lights were on, Aunt Emi had gone to rest for a while, and Auntie Kobe sat in an armchair knitting. Tama was on the rug curled up in front of the fire, dreaming peaceful cat dreams, twitching and purring in sheer pleasure.

Keiko loved to answer the telephone. She loved to say "hello" in big round tones, instead of the short quick *"moshi-moshi"* they used back home.

"Hello," she said now in her best round tones.

There was a short pause and then a man's voice said, "Is that you, Keiko?"

No one but Mike had ever phoned her before. Who in the world could this be? "Yes," Keiko answered quickly. "Yes."

"This is Bob Fletcher."

Keiko got flustered just thinking about Mr. Fletcher, Mike's troop leader and the best writer on the *Richmond Gazette*, calling her up on the telephone! She couldn't think of a thing to say. She gulped and listened, waiting for him to say something more.

"Are you there?" he asked.

Keiko nodded. "Yes," she said again. She wondered if Mr. Fletcher had called to say he was too busy ever to write that story about Jiro. But he hadn't at all.

"I've got somebody here I think you'd all like to see," Mr. Fletcher said.

"It's Jiro-san!" Keiko shouted into the telephone because she knew that's who it must be. "You've found Jiro-san!"

When Auntie Kobe heard that, she dropped all the stitches on the row she was knitting, stepped on Tama's tail, and almost tripped on a chair as she rushed to the telephone.

"Where is he?" she asked breathlessly. "Is Jiro really there? Has someone found him?"

Keiko was too excited to hear another word. "It's Mr. Fletcher," she said, thrusting the telephone at Uncle Henry to let him listen instead. Then she ran in to tell Aunt Emi.

"Mr. Fletcher's found Jiro-san," she called, and then she dashed back to the living room.

Uncle Henry was grinning and nodding as he listened. "Well, by George!" he said. "Well! Yes . . . yes . . . we'll be home. All right."

And then he hung up and said, "Bob did find Jiro-san! He's bringing him right over."

Aunt Emi had come from her room now, and Auntie Kobe began to hug everybody—first Aunt Emi and then Keiko and then she even picked Tama up and hugged her. She didn't hug Uncle Henry though, and he backed off to make sure she wouldn't.

"*Mah,*" Auntie Kobe said over and over again. "I can't believe it. I can't believe I've truly found Jiro." And for once in her life she seemed to be all out of words.

Auntie Kobe hurried to her room to comb her hair and powder her nose, and by the time she came out, Keiko heard a car pull up in front of the house. She ran to the door, turned on the porch light, and peered out into the darkness.

There was Mr. Fletcher, all right, and there was a Japanese man with him. He was shorter than Bob Fletcher, his hair was cropped short, and he was tanned from long years of working in the fields. As he came up the steps, Keiko looked for the scar. Yes, there did seem to be just the faintest trace of a line on his cheek. It was Jiro-san!

He smiled as he saw Keiko, and she liked his firm handshake. "You're Keiko!" he said, as though she didn't know.

"You're Jiro-san!" she said right back to him, grinning.

And then suddenly there was one enormous jumble of confusion as Jiro greeted Auntie Kobe, and everyone was shaking hands and slapping backs and grinning as though they could hardly stand it. And Aunt Emi and Auntie Kobe had to cry because it was all so wonderful.

Keiko herself felt like laughing and crying all at once because she was so excited and happy and proud that she'd helped find Jiro-san.

When everyone had calmed down a little, Mr. Fletcher explained that he'd gone home to visit his mother in Modesto and had told her about Keiko and Jiro and Auntie Kobe because he felt so bad about not having written the story.

"And what do you think?" he went on. "Mother knew Jiro all along. He'd been working on a farm in nearby Livingston and had done some odd jobs for her from time to time."

"She's been a good friend to me," Jiro added. Then he turned to Auntie Kobe and told her how he had hoped for so long to send for her, but had wanted to wait until he had a farm of his own.

"I haven't been much of a success," he said quietly. "Even now I don't have my own land."

"As if that mattered," Auntie Kobe said, dabbing at her eyes again. "Everything will be fine from now on because I'll help."

"I will too," Keiko said, scarcely thinking about what she said.

"You'll have to visit us when we get a farm, and ride the horse and feed the chickens," Jiro said. "We'll have barbecues by the river when it gets warmer," he went on, "and I'll show you how to fish and swim. Nothing will be too good for you, Kei-chan. After all, I wouldn't be here tonight if you hadn't talked to Mr. Fletcher."

"It was really because of Tama," Keiko admitted.

"And Tama wouldn't have gotten lost if Uncle Henry hadn't put her out that night," Aunt Emi added.

It was funny how everything went in circles. Tama wouldn't have been here if Keiko hadn't met Auntie Kobe on the ship, and she wouldn't have been on the ship in the first place if Aunt Emi and Uncle Henry hadn't invited her.

"You see," Aunt Emi said, sounding like Mother, "everything is connected after all."

And we're all connected together now too, Keiko thought. Aunt Emi and Uncle Henry, Auntie Kobe and Jiro-san, Mike and the Michaelsons, and Mr. Fletcher, and Tama, and me . . . everybody. It was like having another family over here, a whole new American family.

Aunt Emi went to the kitchen to put on some hot water for tea, but when it was ready, Uncle Henry wouldn't let her make just plain old green tea.

"This calls for something special," he said, and he brought out two of his best and most beautiful brown tea bowls from their brocade containers. They curved just so, to fit the palm of a hand, and Uncle Henry filled one with tiny scoops of the palest green powdered tea, poured some hot water into it, and then beat it with a small bamboo brush to a light, bubbly froth. He turned the cup around then, just so, lifted it with both hands, and offered the first cup to Jiro.

"Because you have found your mother," he said.

Then he made the second cup for Auntie Kobe. "Because you have found your son."

When they had finished, the cups were washed and Uncle Henry made two more. He gave the first to Mr. Fletcher because he was the one who had actually found Jiro, and the next cup to Keiko.

He smiled as he held it in both hands and bowed as he gave it to her. And he didn't say it was because she had helped to find Jiro. He said simply, "Because you are a good daughter." And then he added, "Someday, when you are older, these cups will be yours, and I shall show you how to make a cup of tea like this too."

Aunt Emi looked at Keiko and smiled as she gave her a little nod.

And Keiko didn't wrinkle her nose or murmur that she was staying only for a year. She thanked Uncle Henry, sipped her tea in a most lady-like manner, and knew now that she had a home in America too.

Glossary

Chan	chahn	Usually added to a child's name. It is a little like calling a boy named Bill, Billy.
Hibachi	hee-bah-chee	a brazier
Kimono	kee-moh-noh	a Japanese dress
Mah	mah	an exclamation, like "My!"
Moshi-moshi	moh-shee moh-shee	the Japanese tele phone "hello"
Sah	sah	an exclamation like "Now!" or "Well!"
San	sahn	Used after a name, it can mean Mr., Mrs., or Miss.
Shoji	sho-jee	a paper-paneled slid-ing door
Sukiyaki	skee-yah-kee	a Japanese dish of meat and vegetables cooked together
Tabi	tah-bee	Japanese socks
Zori	zoh-ree	Japanese sandals

Pronunciation of Proper Names

Emi	eh-mee	Hana	hah-nah
Fuji	foo-jee	Hiro	hee-roh

Hisakazu	hee-sah-kah-zoo	Nikko	
Ito	ee-toh	Maru	nik-koh mah-roo
Jiro	jee-roh	Osaka	oh-sah-kah
Kawai	kah-wah-ee	Sawada	sah-wah-dah
Keiko	kay-koh	Shibuya	shee-boo-yah
Kenbo	ken-boh	Tama	tah-mah
Kobe	koh-beh	Tokyo	toh-kyoh
Kyoto	kyoh-toh	Ueno	oo-eh-noh
Miya-		Yoko-	
gawa	mee-yah-gah-wah	hama	yoh-koh-ha-mah

NOTE: These words should be pronounced without accenting
any of the syllables.